Ruby Heart

The Legend Begins

Book One
The King is Born!

By Marian Webb Betts

Lost Legends Publishing, llc
Anderson, Indiana, USA
mwebbbetts@gmail.com

© 2024 by Marian Webb Betts

All rights reserved solely by the author. The author guarantees all contents are original and do not infringe upon the legal rights of any other person or work.

No part of this book may be reproduced in any form without the permission of the author. The views expressed in this book are not necessarily those of the publisher.

Printed in the United States of America.

ISBN: (print)   979-8-9861136-2-3

Ruby Heart

The Legend Begins

Book One
The King is Born!

By Marian Webb Betts

THE LEGENDS OF RUBY HEART

are dedicate to the loving memory
of my Father and Mother,
Alan and Phyllis Webb
who were pioneer missionaries in South Sudan,
giving over 30 years of service
in Sudan, Ethiopia, and Egypt.
They taught me the art of storytelling.

Acknowledgments

I would like to thank: My sister, Jessie McCallum, who did major studies in Biblical understanding. Allen McCallum, a Presbyterian Pastor and Doctor of Divinity, who researched, edited and corrected where needed to keep events based around the birth, death and resurrection of Jesus as accurate as possible.

Dr. Nellie Arnold, who had the utmost faith in me.

And with a hearty thank you to Caroli Wolfe, my Sister in Faith, without whom a simple story would never have become an amazing series of books!

And to my children, Gillean Dean and Christian Betts, who still cheer me forward!

NOTE: *Conversations that are italicized are either thoughts or telepathic conversations.*

The Prologue

❦

My name is Dillwyn Llewellyn. You will meet me formally in the book, "Time Has Come!" I am an archaeologist, mainly because of a vision or perhaps a dream, that I had in my youth. Whatever it was, it has plagued me all my life - it has shaped my life!

❦

The sky is an inky black void. Stars - millions of them - like tiny crystals reflecting and sparkling in an unseen light, surround me. Distant Galaxies, some like clouds building for a thunderstorm, others like pink and blue scarves waving in a breeze, still others swirling in spirals of amazing colors.

Molten lava weaves among the stars like a fiery caterpillar. It approaches, nearer and nearer until it engulfs me, and I float on its flow within a viscose tunnel through which I can still see the stars beyond.

The caterpillar is drawn toward a massive ball of fire, circling it again and again. One end curls into itself, rolling itself into a ball. Tighter and tighter, the inner walls dissolving, forming a molten lake, churned by the ball's motion.

I can no longer see the stars through the outer wall. Waves of lava splash against the wall and begin to stick, creating ridges and ledges. The pool of lava diminishes as ridges and ledges spread into it, absorbing and solidifying more and more of the lava.

In the pool, crystals begin to form, bobbing on the surface, catching its glow in their prisms. They spin and twirl and dance, and I swear I can hear laughter and singing.

Other objects begin to bob to the surface; lumpy bits of hardening lava, some sinking again, others float a little longer.

One lump about the size of my two fists put together manages to stay afloat and attempts to join the crystals, but they move away. The lump bobs on the surface, all alone. I feel its sorrow.

The King is Born

Suddenly I am ejected out of the forming ball, back into the inky blackness of space. It's cold here, fiercely cold!

I turn toward the warmth of the ball of hardening magma – at least the one from which I'd just been ejected, because I realize it's only one of several that have formed orbits around the giant gas ball.

I watch my planet, for surely that's what it is, as it begins to change colors. Rivers of molten lava occasionally escape the surface, forming giant ridges and deep chasms. The chasms fill with water that erodes the ridges. It flows together to make a mighty ocean surrounding and dividing the ridges. The ridges and hills develop shades and hues of green that turn to yellows, oranges, and golden reds.

At the poles of the planet, the water pales until it becomes white. The white spreads toward the equator, and about the time I think it's going to become a ball of ice, it tilts, and the ice and snow recedes. Once again it turns to shimmering shades of blue, green, yellow and brown.

I have not forgotten that lumpy bit of rock floating alone in the magma. I know this planet I watched being created is Earth, and that the little rock has to be here somewhere. I must go in search of it. A rock the size of my two fists set together cannot be hard to find, surely!

But the planet has aged with the passing of time, and the blue water has eroded the green land, creating rivers, lakes, seas and oceans that break that land into sections stretching, haphazardly the length and breadth of the planet.

I roam the land, avoiding areas where the still molten planet center is trying to push through: volcanoes, lava pits and giant rifts.

Even as I search, the land continues to change. Humans who have been placed here to tend, till and protect the land and all that lives on it are beginning to make their mark on the land.

The sound of an alarm intrudes, and I slowly wake, my thoughts still centered around that rock.

One day, perhaps, I will find out what happened to that rock, the size of my two fists put together.

The Prologue

But, for now, I can't think of a single reason that could tempt me out of the warm cocoon of my bed.

I remember that up in the attic there's still one old trunk to go through. Something is telling me that I must open it, today! Now!

I stop to make a cup of coffee and head to the attic. It's cold up here, the wind moaning and whistling through the old windows, reminding me that it's late October.

"Think I'll take it to the parlor where it's warmer!"

I attempt to lift it, but it weighs a ton. I put my shoulder to a side and shove. It slides to the top of the stairs, teeters there for a second, then tips and bumps its way down the attic stairs.

"No! NO!" I shout as I leap down the stairs after it. It reaches the landing on edge and cartwheels across the upstairs hallway. I make a dive for it as it teeters on the top step of the main staircase. My fingers brush it, the pressure just enough to send it sliding down the stairs with me following on my belly.

I sit up and dust off my butt.

"Well now, wasn't that an adventure!" I hear a man's laughter and a woman's anxious voice.

I must confess I am of Welsh descent and tend to have a fey ability to hear things not of this world. Clairaudient, it's called. I often can hear the voices of those gone before and sometimes other people's thoughts - not always the greatest gift! So, hearing a man's laughter and a woman's voice isn't unusual.

"Glad you enjoyed that!" I quip. "That's the second time you've had a good laugh at my expense!" I stop to look around. "You know what they say about paybacks, don't you?"

"No, I do not. What do they say?"

"They are a - a - well a female dog!"

"This is not supposed to happen! You are not supposed to hear me!" The presence fades away.

I return to the kitchen and make another cup of coffee before pushing the trunk into the parlor and collapsing on a sofa.

"Open! Open!" It's that woman's anxious voice again, the anxiety increased.

The King is Born

I brush my hand across the top of the trunk and feel excitement surge through me.

"Turn of the 19th Century, by the look and feel of it." The old key-lock gives way easily, and the lid rises with a Banshee shriek. I lift out layer upon layer of tissue-wrapped garments, the age increasing as I go.

"Hurry! Hurry!" The voice is frantic.

I swipe at a few bits of tissue.

"Open! Open! Hurry!"

"There's nothing left!" I brush the at the bits again, my knuckles hitting the bottom of the trunk. "That sounds hollow!"

I notice there's a tiny space between the edges of the bottom and the sides. A tiny bit of silk protrudes along the back side. I grab it and pull, exposing a small compartment with a velvet wrapped object in its center and an envelope on top of it. With shaking fingers, I rip open the envelope and carefully unfold a piece of paper. The ink is faded, the handwriting not that of my mother's.

It is written in Italian and reads:

"My name is Marcella Riccio. It is the year 1939. Here in Italy, we watch with trepidation as Mussolini's power and despotism escalates. We are preparing to leave as the anti-Semitic laws he has instituted have forced many of our friends to flee ahead of deportation to camps. It may not be long until even we Christians will be attacked. Fear is rampant.

"I am hiding Ruby in the false bottom of this trunk. She will be safe until her next Custodian finds her."

It is signed, Marcella Riccio, of the family of Josias, Grandson of Basilikos, out of Balthazar, Clan of Madjid.

"Josias, Grandson of Basilikos! That was the writer of the scrolls I discovered in a cave in Wales!"

"Open! Open!" The voice is loud in my head.

"OK, OKaay!" I hurriedly put the letter down and unfold old velvet to expose a beautiful enameled, jewel-encrusted jewelry box. I carefully lift it and set it on the coffee table, kneeling to inspect the box closer.

"OPEN!"

THE PROLOGUE

It's almost a yell in my head. My hands shake as I flip the catch and turn toward the light of the setting sun. The lid opens and brilliant beams of red flash and swirl, filling the room. I gasp and almost drop the box. In the swirling lights I see glimpses of people, places, a baby, camels, a citadel, a cross. Emotions swirl, swell, and recede. Voices, laughter, tears, agony.

The light gathers and pours through the window, filling the whole view with golden red light and joyous song.

I sink to the floor and set the box on the coffee table, closing my eyes.

"I'm free! I'm free! Oh, it is so good to see!"

"Ruby? Ruby, it is you!" It's that man's voice again. "You are a poet and you did not know it!"

"Mongke! OH!! It is so good to hear your voice!"

"And yours, too Ruby!"

"Where are you?" The voices are so clear, surely, they aren't in my head!

"Is this our new Custodian ? She's quite pretty, even dressed like a boy!"

The man laughs. "It is the 21st Century, Ruby. Women dress like men and men like women!"

"Who is talking? " I demand.

"My name is Ruby. Ruby Heart. I exist in the gemstone in the box." The female voice responds.

I gingerly lift the lacy golden pendant from its velvet bed. It just fits in palm of my hand. As I raise it closer I see a gemstone inside, a ruby which is roughly shaped like a human heart. The sun glints once again on its facets and a vision appears:

A sea of lava and an ugly little stone floating by itself in the waves.

"I was created as the planet we call earth was still in liquid form. I remember it as if it were yesterday."

"You were in that rock! That rock I saw floating in the lava in my dream! That rock I have spent my life trying to find!"

Chapter One
In the Beginning

At Ruby's suggestion, I have rearranged a small sitting room so that the furniture all faces one blank wall. I place Ruby on the coffee table near the fireplace where the firelight can touch her then settle in a comfortable chair watching as the light catches in Ruby and spills out. At first it dances around the room as if joyously freed from a long time hidden.

Ruby draws the light back into herself, then beams it against the wall and begins to tell her story.

Before Time Began

You have already heard of me from Dillwyn, my 21st Century Custodian . I will take you back to the pool of lava inside the forming planet, now called Earth where I float to the surface of the pool of lava. I'm drawn to the sound of voices raised in laughter and song and move to join other crystals dancing on the waves of lava. But they reject me and shoo me away.

"Ugly rock! Yuk!"

"Maybe it thinks it's a beautiful crystal like us! Te-he-he!"

I float alone on the waves, their laughter growing faint.

"Creator, why don't they like me? Why do they say I'm ugly?" My voice is young and innocent.

"Ruby, you are more beautiful than ten of them! You are special. But I have hidden your beauty within a rock until time comes."

"Who is Time? And why do I have to wait for them?"

"Time is not a being, Ruby," Creator chuckles. *"But you will understand - in time."*

The King is Born
1,000 BC

The rock in which I've been embedded seems to come alive, throwing me in every direction possible as rock-splintering sounds break the silence of ions.

I whimper in fear.

"Be still, Ruby. Time is coming!"

"Creator?" My voice quavers. *"Is that Time I hear?"*

"No, Ruby," on a chuckle. *"That is water you hear. It will free you from the rock in which you have hidden for so long. It will free you for my purpose. Time will come!"*

The water does free me - in time. And for a very long time, the rock that encased me has lane at the bottom of the Oxus River. Minnows swim over and around my rock. The sun warms my rock by day, welcome after a long cold night.

500 BC

There's commotion along the bank of the river.

"Time has come, Ruby!"

I'm alert, listening to the sounds coming closer.

"Is that Time, Creator?"

Metal scraping on rock sounds close by. My rock is jostled, tossed and rolled about.

"It is a Human, Ruby. I want him to pick you."

In my excitement, I try to jump up and down.

"Pick me! Pick me!" I yell, though I know it can't hear me. To my amazement, it picks me.

"It picked me, Creator!" Wonder. *"Does it talk?"* Curious.

"His name is Cutter. He will free you from the rock. And, yes, he talks." A chuckle. *"But not so you can understand yet. You will, in time."*

"There's that time thing again!" I pout.

Chapter One - In the Beginning

On a plateau high above the Oxus River, a village of thatched, mud and wattle huts surrounds a lake with an artesian spring bubbling up in its center.

Cutter approaches a hut and opens the door. Inside, he lights an oil lamp and dumps out the contents of his pouch, sweeping all aside except for my rock.

"Not much to look at, are you? Let's see what's inside."

Taking a chisel and hammer he lightly taps my rock, breaking a chuck off.

"Ouch! That hurts!" I wince. *"Creator! Make it stop!"*

With a grunt of satisfaction, he chips at the rest of the rock.

Finally, he stops chipping and takes my now cleaned body out of the vice, holding me close to the lamp. With another grunt he rubs me with something lovely and soft.

"That feels good. Oh, don't stop!" As he takes me with him through the door into the sunlight.

It's noisy out here. Two-wheeled carts trundle by. Hawkers in stalls set up along the lake's bank yelling their wares. People coming and going. I cringe from the unfamiliar noise.

Cutter crosses the street and finds a quiet place by the lake shore to examine me, lifting me to the light.

I gasp with astonishment. *"Creator! I can see again! THAT's a human? Oh, the blue heavens! And what -"*

"Beautiful! Magnificent! The colors - the fire! Yes! You will make a magnificent gift!"

I ignore the voice of the man and bask in the delightfully warm sunshine. My cleaned facets soak up the light, gathering it into a pool within me. Without warning, the lights shoots out through my facets in all directions, drawing the attention of the passersby. They gather around Cutter, eager to see what he's found.

"What's it saying, Creator?"

"He says you are beautiful, magnificent."

"That can't be right! The others said -"

"And I told you that they didn't know your inner beauty! Now you will shine!"

The King is Born

The people are grabbing for me, crying out in anguish, some determined they must have me! They push and pull at Cutter.

A shadow blocks the sun as something snatches me out of Cutter's fingers.

It rises high in the air, passes the edge of the plateau.

"Creator! Something has taken me from Cutter!" I squeal in fear.

"Golden Eagle won't hurt you. Look between his talons and enjoy and learn. You are safe."

Through the Golden Eagle's talons, I look down at the panorama below.

Streams meander through the broad valley, sometimes wide and slow, sometimes narrow and deep, sometimes shallow, sparkling in the bright sunshine, gurgling, chattering and laughing.

Gazelles, wild asses and red deer graze the fresh green grass, their young frolicking fearlessly among them.

Hares scurry to hide from a honey badger working its way through the valley, nose to ground, scratching and snuffling as it goes.

Golden Eagle rises on the thermals, breasting cliffs, soaring over plateaus where herds of red deer and Markhors - a wild goat species with twisted horns - graze.

Continuing our ascent, Golden Eagle carries me above the foothills of the Pamir Mountains, swooping low, skimming through trees, over rocky outcrops and across green meadows, giving me glimpses of brown bears and their cubs.

Higher still we rise, the air thinning and growing colder. Mountain Goats watch us from their rocky outcrops. A Snow Leopard pauses to glance our way.

Still higher. Far to the south the massive mountain ranges of the Hindu Kush seem to float in the clouds.

Gleaming glaciers swim below us as we crest the mountain tops. I shiver with the cold, then let out a squawk as Golden Eagle tips a wing, almost brushing the snow as it slowly turns and begins a dive between two ridges. Below, the melting glaciers form rivulets that rush and gurgle over the rocky terrain.

Chapter One - In the Beginning

Golden Eagle flies just above the water which suddenly drops away and we are falling with the downdraft. The thunder of the falling water obliterates all other sounds, including my screams.

Golden Eagle slows its descent, then gently rises as it follows the river down through the foothills. It rises above a cliff. A village comes into view. Golden Eagle approaches a group of people. One turns at the sound of the eagle's approach.

"It's the human!" I gasp. Golden Eagle opens its talons. I'm falling.

"Achhhhhhhk!"

Cutter catches me, and, pressing me tightly against his robe, and begins to move. There's a loud thud - not of stone, but lighter, deeper - followed by a rattle and another thud. Cutter is breathing hard and fast, his chest heaving against me. I can still hear the voices clamoring:

"I want to see it again!"

"I just want to hold it!"

"I must have it!"

"I'll pay you anything -"

Cutter returns to his work bench and lays me on it. I watch with curiosity as he forms a thin, golden cage around me and hangs me on a chain. With another satisfied grunt, he lays me back on the table and steps out of the room.

"Ruby, it will not be long now until you face the first task I have for you."

"What is it, Creator? I can't wait to find out!"

"Cutter is going to present you to his leader."

"Yes! Yes! You told me -"

"Do not interrupt me!" Sternly. *"Do you remember when the sun shone through you?"*

Afraid to speak, I tremble on the bench.

"I was testing you. You responded well."

Cutter returns and wraps me in a something soft and drops me, the fall cut short and I'm swinging back and forth.

THE KING IS BORN

Creator continues to speak. *"I have a very important message for you to give to Cutter's Chief. It means life or death - "*

"What's life or death?" My mind is on overload, and I forget Creator had told me not to interrupt Him.

Creator groans as Cutter picks up the bag I'm in and heads out the door.

Chapter Two
A Child is Taken

Cutter joins others who greet him boisterously. Laughter and raised voices abound. The group heads toward the Gathering Hall, a tall, long, thatched building across a small lake from a white marble temple glimmering in the evening light.

The men enter the Hall, calling greetings to others already seated at spread out between two rows of columns supporting the roof lost in the smoking fire brands set in scones on the columns. Oil lamps stand on each table.

At the far end, is a single table where the leaders of the village sit.

A gong sounds, and the men lurch to their feet as Xanthos, the Head Men and High Priest of the clan enters and is seated in the center of the head table.

As the men settle once again, servants bring in heavy trays of food. Others pour wine from large earthen jugs. The merriment increases. Once the first trays are removed, a servant approaches Xanthos with a bundle in his arms. Xanthos rises and takes the bundle, carefully unwrapping it to expose a newly born baby boy. Bereft of its swaddling clothes, the baby squalls and squirms. Xanthos raises him high above his head.

"My son, Euphraino! Rejoice! For a son is born!"

The men rise and cheer, raising their goblets in a salute. As they return to their seats, several begin to line up to present gifts for the baby. Cutter is second in line.

"Ruby, listen carefully! Cutter is about to present you to Xanthos. When you are lifted up to the light, show him the vision I am giving you."

Cutter approaches the table and removes my golden cage from its pouch, presenting me in the palm of his hand.

The King is Born

Xanthos takes the chain, lifting me to eye level. I swing and dance with excitement, catching the light of the torches. Xanthos is transfixed.

"Now, Ruby!" Creator shouts.

Xanthos gasps in surprise as he sees the banquet hall in my facets.

However, the banquet is over. Men are relaxing around the tables, some still drinking, others attempting to do so. Several are slumped across the tables.

The pounding of boots on cobblestones intrudes. The hall doors shake as they are pummeled. They splinter and fly open, crashing against the walls. Figures in warrior garb surge through, tossing flaring torches and brandishing scimitars.

The warrior's howls are answered by shouts at the men as they rise - or attempt to rise, toppling the tables, the oil lamps crashing to the straw on the floor and igniting it. The overturned tables are shoved into the oncoming hoard and skitter back with the force of the numbers.

Flames in the straw on the floor pause for only seconds as mud and wattle walls ignite. The scene dissolves in fire and smoke.

In the banquet hall, Xanthos, his face white as a ghost, jumps to his feet, reaching for his short sword with a shout of warning.

Instantly, all voices stop, the men freezing in place.

The silence is deafening.

Xanthos looks toward the closed doors, and around the room at the frozen men.

No wild-eyed barbarians. No fire. The tables are in place.

Sheepishly, Xanthos sheaths his sword and thanks Cutter for his beautiful gift. Cutter clasps it around Xanthos' neck and moves on.

"Did I do in right, Creator?"

"Yes, Ruby. You did well. He saw the vision. But we must wait to see if he understood it."

Chapter Two - A Child is Taken

The night is far spent, the platters have been removed, the jugs left on the tables. Several men are slumped over the tables while others attempt to fill their goblets or drink from them. A few are still lively. Chatter, laughter, clinking goblets merge into a gentle hum in the low light of the smoking torches.

A commotion breaks out: leather slapping on cobblestones, clashing swords, war-hoops.

Heads lift. Faces turn. Bodies rise. Doors smash open. Giant shadowy figures rush in, wielding flashing blades.

Men are on their feet, fumbling for their swords. Benches crash. Tables skitter across the floor. Lamps shatter, splashing burning oil. Fire runs up the walls. Hungry flames lick, catch hold, devouring.

Yells. Screams. Clashing steel.

Smoke swirls, parts momentarily to show Xanthos, shrouded in a black cloak, grabbing the baby and heading for a back door.

Outside, he wastes no time looking back at the building now engulfed in flames.

Running. Hiding – a shadow scuttling among shadows, heading for the temple only a hundred yards away!

"Temple! Safety!" Gasping.

Horses' hooves pound on turf. Xanthos glances over his shoulder. Two riders are racing toward him. Xanthos mounts the temple steps, turning triumphantly.

"Sanctuary!"

The horses clatter up the steps. One rider snatches the baby.

"No! No! Not the child, please!" Xanthos wails, holding out his empty arms.

The second rider swings his scimitar, Xanthos' head sails through the air, landing in the lake with a loud splash. On shore, the lifeless body slithers down the steps and into the water. I land with a final plop between the head and the body.

Across the lake the skeletal remains of the Hall collapse into the hungry flames. Smoke swirls over the scene.

"That wasn't supposed to happen, was it?"

THE KING IS BORN

"No. But the child is safe."

"What's a child?"

"Oh, Ruby! You have so much to learn! But for now, you must stay hidden here in the lake. Time will come again."

Chapter Three
The Results of A Ritual

The events Ruby had shown me in that first evening have stayed with me, the shock of the ending lingering for several days. The Archaeologist in me wants to know more about the people and their lifestyle, buildings and events. And Ruby is happy to oblige.

"Tonight I'm going to show you an event that doesn't seem to relate in any way, but eventually you will understand."

"In time," I laugh. "I know!"

Ruby chuckles as a moonlit night appears on the wall.

430 BC

A full moon rides high above a wide valley, its light revealing a large, trampled area surrounded by a circle of black caped figures. In the center of this circle stands an angry white Brahma bull. Moonlight reflects off dark streaks running down its flanks. Some arrows are still embedded in its skin.

A lone man dressed in a short white tunic, steps into the ring, facing the bull. The moonlight glimmers on the sharp steel of the short sword in his hand.

The bull lowers its head and charges. The man sidesteps aside, thrusting his sword into the bull's neck. The bull's horn impales the man, the bull tossing him high in the air as it drops to its knees and slowly sinks to the ground, and topples to one side. The man's body lands close to it, a groan issuing from its mouth.

The shadowed figures melt into the night, leaving the two bodies where they fell.

I'm stunned. "Ruby, the other night's visions were bad enough! Do we have to see more of this?"

"Keep watching. It gets better."

The King is Born

The moon is waning now. Human figures dressed in saffron robes approach the scene and stop.

One squats beside the man's body then beckons the others. They lift the body, holding it off the ground as the first monk wraps its midriff with his own robe and spreads a second robe on the ground.

The men lay the body on the robe and tie the corners to some of their staffs. The procession returns the way it had come, heading along an unseen path that winds through valleys, rising higher into the mountains. It approaches a cliff face and doesn't stop moving, seeming to walk right through the rock.

We follow the procession through the cliff into a large cavern. A cheerfully crackling fire in a central large fire pit creates dancing shadows that merge, hiding both the walls and the ceiling.

The monks place the man's body near the fire and step back.

I realize the firelight is not the only light in the massive cavern. High on the walls opposite, large, arched windows let in the moonlight that creates sliver paths running toward the fire pit.

A sharp cry - more a bleat - precedes the appearance of a deformed figure shrouded in an oversized cape that emerges from the shadows, hobbles to the inert figure, and throws itself on the body. The sounds it's making is that of a sheep or goat in distress.

A man in a long white robe appears striding down one of the moonbeam paths. The gathered figures part to let him through. He lifts the distraught figure, holding him against his own chest, comforting it as he would a child.

After some time, the man sets the little figure down, patting it before turning to the still figure. He lifts it with ease and walks through the crowd along the moonbeam from which he had appeared, and disappeared through the outer wall of the cavern.

In the moonlight, the valley slumbers on between its impenetrable cliffs.

෴♥෴

Chapter Four
Ruby is Found

෴♥෴

"I hope there's no bloodshed tonight, Ruby!" I warn as I settle to watch another segment of Ruby's story.

"No worries! Tonight you get to meet several new people. I will explain who they are as they appear in the story."

34 BC

A solitary man stops on a low rise above what I recognize to be the Oxus River. He is mounted on what appears to be a camel.

"That is Madjid. Are you familiar with the Bactrian camel?"

"No. I noticed it looks very different from the camels I have ridden."

"The Bactrian camel is more suited for the higher elevations of the Hindu Kush. It has two humps and is covered by long, dark hair with a thick undercoat. It's attitude and behavior is no better than the Dromedary you mentioned.

"Madjid, like you, is interested in things of the past. Today, he has two purposes on his mind: to find the remains of a legendary temple, and, more pragmatically, to locate a new home for his growing clan."

A caravan toils behind him along the road from Bactra, that ancient city whose walls spread across the desert hills south of the Oxus River (now the Amu Daria that flows north from the mountains to the Aral Sea).

To the east, the rolling sand dunes give way to cliffs that sweep up into the Hindu Kush. To the south is the junction of two rivers that form the Oxus. A perpetual mist rising from the waters, glinting now in the bright sunshine, surrounds the base of a central rock buttress upon which stand the remnants of a marble wall, a remnant of a temple that once stood there.

The King is Born

In the early morning mists rising from the conjoining rivers, the scene looks less substantial than the gossamer green fronds hanging over the walls of Bactra.

"That's it!"

"My Lord?" Josias, Madjid's servant has caught up with him.

"There! Above the mist, just as they said."

"Do you think the legends are true?" Hesitant.

"We will find out! I'm going on ahead. Bring the others after me. There appears to be a break that may give us access to the bluff."

"Very well my Lord. But. Should you go alone?"

"Father! Let me come with you!" A camel pulls to a stop on Madjid's other side. Its rider is a youth of about fourteen, bright blue eyes, flushed cheeks. Madjid smiles.

"All right, Balthazar, why not! But first, find your mother and bring her to me. I'm going on ahead." He spurs his camel to an easy lope and disappears over the rise. Balthazar turns back to the caravan. Josias hesitates, then follows his master.

Madjid arrives across from the break he had seen earlier - on the other side of the river, dismounts and hands his reigns to Josias who follows him as he searches along the riverbank for a place to cross.

Balthazar and his mother soon join them, and the four cross the river. They work their way along a runnel of water up to the plateau.

Madjid's wife, Issaca taps her camel to kneel, dismounts, and stoops to scoop water from the stream, sipping it.

"The water is good!" She splashes water over her face, then encourages her camel to rise and drink. She tethers him to the branch of a decimated tree and settles on a rock in the little shade it offers, removing her shawl and closing her eyes.

Madjid dismounts, tethers his camel and crosses the stream.

Balthazar slides off his camel and begins to explore the stream bed, too. His untethered camel wanders off in search of grass.

"Up the gully on this side." Issaca's eyes are still closed. Madjid recrosses the stream and offers her his hand.

Chapter Four - Ruby is Found

"Let's go, then!"

"My camel!" Cries Balthazar.

"Let that be a lesson, Balthazar! Go find it and catch up with us."

"How'd you do that, Mother?" Balthazar asks as he catches up with them.

"You close your eyes and empty your mind of all thought. It will come."

"You must learn the ways of your mother, Balthazar. If you prove to have the Sight it could be very helpful when you join the priesthood."

"But, Father, I am your heir. Don't you want me to produce heirs, also?"

"You have many brothers," Madjid glances at his wife and continues in a whisper. "We'll discuss this at another time, Balthazar. We're here!"

Issaca reaches the plateau first, stopping to take in the view. As far as she can see to the southeast, tall, dry grasses undulate in a gentle breeze. To the north, a few stunted treetops peep above the grass. She heads for the trees.

Near the trees lies a boggy pond surrounded by bulrushes and reeds.

The three tether the camels in the shade and spread out to explore. Balthazar heads toward the ruined wall that they had seen from the valley. Madjid goes to investigate some promising grass-covered mounds. Issaca finds an animal trail that leads to open water and notices an occasional disturbance in the water near the center of the pond. Something glitters in the depths close to the bubbling water. As she focuses on the glitter, it grows brighter. Suddenly, it flashes rays of blood-red light.

With a cry, Issaca claps her hands over her face and eyes.

"Madjid! Madjid! It's here!" Madjid hurries to her side. "The Vision! It happened here!"

"Say! Look at this! These walls are marble! This must have been the temple! It won't take much -" he glances toward his parents. "What's the matter?"

THE KING IS BORN

"It happened here!!" Madjid shouts with excitement.

"What happened here?"

"Your mother's visions!"

Balthazar is running toward his parents when two riders appear, racing toward him. He drops to a crouch, unsheathing his short sword. The riders pass him, heading for the ruined wall. As quickly as they appeared, they vanished.

Balthazar rises slowly from the crouch and looks around the plateau, shading his eyes with his hand.

"What have you seen?" Madjid.

Balthazar sheaths his sword and joins his father.

"Two horsemen heading for the temple."

"You saw them?" Issaca. "Then I'm right. This is the place!"

Balthazar investigates the pool at his mother's feet. Fire flickers in its depths. He grips his mother's hand. "We have to empty the pool!"

They return to the caravan and lead it further up into the hills, finding a way back down onto the plateau. The rest of the day is spent setting up camp.

༄༅༄༅

The following day Madjid joins Balthazar by the pond. Two of Madjid's brothers, Kasim and Hiram stand a little way behind them, talking quietly.

"Why has no one attempted to rebuild here? It's so well positioned." Hiram.

"He will not allow it!" Magus Darius in priestly robes, joins them, followed by Issaca in the formal white robes of a Prophetess.

"Who is he?" Hiram.

"The High Priest who was murdered on the temple steps." Darius.

"I thought it was the Chief!" Hiram, confused. "What god did they worship?"

Darius shrugs. "Not our God." He turns to sweep his arm across the whole area. "We will destroy what's here, cleanse the grounds and build to our God whose name is too sacred to say."

Chapter Four - Ruby is Found

"No." Balthazar speaks with an authority not heard in him before.

Darius spins toward him, his face suffused with rage.

"First we empty the pool," Balthazar. "THEN, we will cleanse the grounds and build our temple."

"Who are you to speak against my orders?!"

Issaca steps between the Magus and her son.

"The young prophet has spoken. Hear him!"

"He's nothing but a lad!" Blusters Darius. "No learning in the arts. Unproven!"

The two face each other: Magus Darius' robes trembling with his rage; the prophetess calm, her chin up, eyes serene.

"He proved himself last night. We will listen to him." Madjid turns to his son. "Balthazar, how do you propose we empty the pool?"

The men move together around Balthazar. Issaca moves to the edge of the pool, Darius joining her and bending close.

"I don't appreciate your attempt to usurp my authority!" A harsh whisper.

"I wasn't attempting anything." She continues to study the pond. "You would do well to pay attention to young Balthazar. If you are smart, you will get him into the Priesthood quickly. He will become Magus of the tribe of Madjid."

Darius, sneering. "The Prophetess speaks?" Raising his voice, "What's this about the tribe of Madjid? Since when? This is still the tribe of Jenghiz!"

Issaca heads to join the men, speaking over her shoulder as she goes.

"Jenghiz is dead. Madjid rules!"

Darius spits on the ground. "Paah!" He strides down the hill, muttering to himself.

⊙♥☙

The reeds and rushes have been cleared away, the artesian spring capped with a large stone. The head of the stream has also been cleared and deepened, allowing the water is drain away quit.

THE KING IS BORN

Nearby an awning has been erected where most of the men rest. Hiram joins Balthazar as he wanders through the mounds of dirt that had caught his father's attention on arrival. Hiram's path takes him back to the pond first. He stops abruptly, staring into the muddy remains of the pond.

"Balthazar! Madjid! You better come see this!"

Balthazar and Madjid join him, looking where he points. The rib cage of a skeleton protrudes from the mud.

"Where's the skull?" Madjid.

"Over there!" Balthazar points to the skull a few feet away, close to the artesian fountainhead. He begins to pull off his robes.

"What are you doing?!" Madjid.

"There's something . . ." Puzzled. "I must find it!" He hands his outer garments to his father and pulls his tunic between his legs, tucking it in his sash.

"What can I do to help?"

Balthazar steps into the mud and instantly slips. Madjid catches him and steadies him.

"I guess you can try and keep me on my feet!" Grinning.

Madjid grimaces. "Yah! Sure!"

༄༅༄

The sun is just inches from the horizon.

Balthazar, looking more like a mud monster than human, grunts with satisfaction and straightens, studying what's in his hand while stretching his aching back.

"You've found something?" Madjid returns to the water's edge.

Balthazar holds his hand up for his father to help him out. Madjid grimaces and mutters as he grasps Balthazar's hand, his eyebrows rising in surprise at his son's strong grip.

"When did you get so strong?" He wonders to himself.

Issaca joins them, slightly breathless. "What did you find, Balthazar? Let me see it!"

Balthazar turns to his mother. His embarrassment is plain to see. Madjid throws a cloak over his shoulders.

Chapter Four - Ruby is Found

Balthazar quickly pulls it around him as he speaks.

"Mother! I was going to come to you as soon as I got cleaned up. It's him!"

"I know that!" Impatient. "What else?"

"I need a bucket of water."

A bucket is brought. He plunges his hands in it, gently rocking them back and forth loosening the dirt. When the dirt's gone, he raises his hands, opening them to see a golden chain and cage with something inside. He holds the cage up between thumb and a finger for them all to see what is inside: a human heart shaped, red ruby.

"Time has come again, Creator?"

"Yes, Ruby. Time has come again, and your journey has now begun in earnest!"

Chapter Five
Basil's Story Begins

11BC

A magnificent walled city named after the leader of the clan that settled it, now spreads across much of the plateau. On the cliff side, the palace rises two stories. In front of it spreads the lake, its artesian spring now bubbling over the rim of a massive clay jar. Around the lake weeping willows and paths dissect lawns shaded by fruit trees and date palms. Surrounding this, and connecting to the palace walls is a promenade under high, arched colonnades. Shops and small businesses, open to the promenade, are doing a brisk trade.

The sound of children's laughter draws attention to a side street and a gate that opens onto a courtyard - an expanse of stonework, surrounded on three sides by the usual colonnades which, in turn, shades open doorways.

The courtyard is filled with noisy boys enjoying their morning free time.

I am Basilikos - Basil to my friends - the son of Balthazar, grandson of Issaca and Madjid. I seem to have inherited some of Issaca's special powers - second site, for instance. When I touch someone, or when they touch me, I often see something that could happen in the future.

All of the children belong to the Clan of Madjid. My closest friends are sons of my Father's half-brothers, Kasim and Hiram. Gaius, Nicias and Demetris. Thales and his tag-along, Dinias, are also Grandsons of Madjid's brothers. Thales is a brute and a bully. His only followers are those afraid of reprisal.

We are playing tag - which means avoiding being tackled by Thales - when the school bell rings, ending our morning break.

The King is Born

But Thales who is 'it', ignores the bell and barrels into me, knocking me to the ground.

"TAG! You're it!" He runs to a safe distance before turning to jeer at me.

"You're weak, Basilikos! The girls could run faster than you. Oh! Oh!" He mimics a girl's voice. "I hurt my ankle. Oh, my! I think I'm going to faint!" He put the back of his hand to his forehead and sinks to the ground.

"Fine!" I yell in frustration, rubbing my throbbing ankle. "Just wait 'til you break your leg!"

"Come on, Basil," Nicias puts out a hand to help him up. "Pay no attention to them!"

"Yeah!" Gaius agrees.

"I'm all right!" I ignore the offered hand. "Even if it were broken, I wouldn't give him the satisfaction of seeing you help me up!"

Thales follows us into the classroom still taunting me. The teacher scolds him with resignation.

୨୧୨୧

My prediction that day panned out a few weeks later, as we were riding in the hills above Madjid. A groomsmen assigned to teach us how to ride and hunt is leading the way. We ride three abreast on the wide cart road until the groomsman leads us into a canyon where the track is single file.

The going is slow. Thales pushes ahead to be first in line behind the groomsman. It's not long before he gets impatient and orders the groomsman to speed up. Ignoring him, the groomsman stops, pointing across the stream beside us.

"You have all jumped smaller streams before, but this span is wider. Watch how I handle my horse to jump this stream."

"I've done this a hundred times! I don't need you to show me how!' Thales begins to back his horse.

"Thales! Don't do it!" I shout, remembering the vision. But Thales ignores me and pushes his horse to jump. The horse barely makes the jump, its hind hooves only half landing on solid ground. It tips backward, whinnying in fear.

Chapter Five - Basil's Story Begins

Thales loses his grip and falls backwards, screaming, into the stream below. Without Thales' extra weight, the horse manages to save itself.

But Thales isn't so lucky. He starts to get up and falls back onto the rocky stream bed, clutching his broken leg, squalling.

"You hexed me, Basil! It's your fault! You'll pay for this!"

Chapter Six
Fixing a Broken Leg

ೂ♥♥ೞ

I'm studying in Grandmother Issaca's herbal room when she and my mother, Rachel, enters.

"Basilikos! I am on the way to set Thales' leg. I want you to come with me."

I hang my head and refuse to move from the desk.

"What's the matter, Basil?" She asks sharply.

"He thinks I hexed him," mumbled.

"What!" Mother.

"Aw!" I throw my hands in the air, jump up, heading for the door. But Mother catches my arm, pulling me to a stop beside her.

"What happened?" Sharply.

"We were playing tag, and he shoved me to the ground." Head down. "He called me a girl. I told him he wouldn't laugh when he broke his leg."

"And he believes you put a curse on him?!" Rachel.

"Did you?" Issaca.

"NO!" I meet her gaze. "But I did know he would do it one day."

"That's not surprising!" Mother, on a sigh. "As rough and tumble as he is, that would be a good guess by anyone!" She lets me go and takes a few steps before turning back to study me. "What are we going to do with you, Basil?"

"He's no different than his father was at that age," Issaca, crossing to the open door.

"That may be, Mother Issaca," Mother, picks up her basket and follows Grandmother out the door. I tag along. "But Basil has alienated himself from all his cousins. They are afraid of him!"

The King is Born

"You think they are afraid of me, Mother?" A little too sharply. "They laugh and tease me continually. If that is what you call fear –"

"Have respect for you mother, Basilikos!" Father's voice makes me jump.

"Hello, Balthazar!" Issaca sounds not the least surprised. "We were just talking about you."

"Harumph!" He turns to me. "What's this about fear?'

"I meant no disrespect to Mother, Father," I duck my head.

"It seems Thales has fallen off his pony and broken his leg," Issaca.

"I am aware of that. What has that to do with Basilikos?"

"Thales believes he put a curse on him," Issaca.

"Did you?" Father's eyes sharpen with interest.

"No, Father, that's just what I was saying. I just knew it was going to happen."

Father continues to study me. I try not to squirm under those deep blue eyes just like Grandmother's and mine. Finally, he turns to Issaca.

"Mother, are you on your way to Thales now?"

"We are." Issaca.

"Good! I will come with you!" He opens the gate. "We will do this together."

I follow them out the gate into the labyrinth of hallways.

"Walk with me, Basilikos." Father commands. "If you knew that Thales was going to break his leg, why didn't you try to stop him?"

"Me stop Thales, Father? You've got to be joking!" A sharp glance from Father. "Sorry. I didn't know how or when or why it would happen, just that it would."

"Well. He's too big for a pony, anyway. Very soon now you all will go through the Rite of Passage and move into the young men's court. You all will be too busy with more manly pursuits. He won't have time to bother with you then."

Chapter Six - Fixing a Broken Leg

We pass through the children's courtyard into the boys rooms and find Thales sitting up chatting with some of the other boys, his injured leg supported by pillows.

"Thales!" Father calls on entering the room. Instantly, Thales falls back on his pillows, throwing his arm over his face.

"I hear you fell off your pony and broke your leg!"

Thales raises his arm and peers at Father.

"Magus Balthazar?" Pathetically. "Is it really you? Oh, how kind. Thank you for coming to me. So -" moans "- gracious."

Thales lowers his arm and sees Grandmother and Mother, and behind them, me. Instantly, his visage turns to one of hate. His hand moves in a sign to ward off evil. I purposely let a smile curl my lips.

The women prepare to set Thales' leg. Mother offers Thales a flat, smooth wooden paddle to put between his teeth.

"Thales, bite down on this as we set your leg."

"That's for sissies." Thales waves it away. "Men don't need things like that!"

The women glance at each other. Grandmother shrugs. Each one takes hold of Thales leg, one above, the other below the compound fracture. They pull hard and fast. There's a grinding and a click. But it was lost in Thales screams - like a little girl!

I burst out laughing, earning a glare from Father.

Chapter Seven
Learning the Stars

☙❧

When the nights are clear and still, we wrap ourselves in heavy woolen capes and, armed with rugs and furs, go up to the flat rooftop that has waist high walls. It's an excellent place to read the stars. We spread the rugs and skins on the floor and lie on our backs, pulling more rugs over us to keep warm. No lights from the courtyards beneath us penetrate the inky black sky with its dusting of stars so bright it feels like I can reach out and scoop them up.

Father has prepared me well for these nights, having shown me charts of the stars with the names of the constellations. He is a consummate storyteller, and I am an avid student and have quickly learned to recognize the constellations and to repeat the legends of the gods, their adventures and the intrigue that surrounded them.

On this night he surprises me.

"The stars make music," he said. "One of my fondest wishes is to hear that."

"How could they make music, Father?"

"When the Mighty One first created the material and spiritual world, he created all things that are light and good. But the Evil One, the Child of Doubt, created a counter material world of darkness and evil, which is slowly taking over the light and good. In the beginning, you could hear a star and see the wind, but now you can only see the stars and hear the wind."

"But in the end times the good and light will win. Right Father? That's what Ruby tells me, and also the other Magi."

"Yes. At the end, there will be a Day of Judgment. The drink of immortality will be offered to those who have fought against the Evil One and a new creation will be established."

"Will we hear the stars and see the wind then?"

The King is Born

"Yes, so we are told. But there are those who say they have already heard the stars."

"Father, there are many other religions that speak of a creation. Do any of them say anything about the stars singing?"

"Your mother's people, the Israelites believe it. It is mentioned in one of their stories about a man named Job. Job had spoken rashly, questioning Elohim - that is one of the names they have for their god - as to his wisdom and understanding. Elohim answered him from a terrible storm. He asked Job where was he when he - Elohim - made the universe, while all the stars in the heavens sang together and the angels shouted for joy."

"I'd like to hear more of that story."

"Ask your mother sometime. You should be hearing her stories, too. They are as much of your heritage as are mine. Learn what you can from our women - your grandmother and mother. They are not like other women."

"I will."

"Now, come. Let's go down to our beds. The chill is getting into my bones."

Chapter Eight
A Premonition

It's mid-afternoon in late Spring and is already hot and dry. We sit at our desks pretending to work while our teacher, an elderly man who tends to nap after lunch, struggles to keep awake. It's not long until he loses the battle and slumps over his desk, snoring.

Quietly, we slip off our shoes and tiptoe out of the room, across the courtyard to an unused corner where a hidden door opens onto a back alley that leads to an abandoned part of the city. The silence here is almost complete, the shimmering, whitewashed walls blocking the city sounds. A cat, stretched in the shade of a scrawny bush, opens one eye to watch us pass. A dog, flopped on a stoop, manages a low growl.

At the end of the lane, we slip through a low, gated arch in a wall. Here, roofless, dilapidated buildings follow an equally dilapidated aqueduct that runs down a slope to an opening in the outer wall of the city where the water cascades down a short cliff into a pond at its base.

The aqueduct is still covered with slabs of stone intended to keep animals and children out of them. But, in the past, we've managed to push a couple slabs far enough off so that we can get into the sluice. If you lie flat with your arms to your sides, the water will carry you along, gathering speed, the excitement mounting in the dark of the aqueduct. Every sound echoes back and all sense of direction is lost as your body twists and turns. Then, suddenly you shoot out of the aqueduct and drop to the pond below.

As I grip a corner of a slab I see a fleeting an image: water washing over a body caught in the aqueduct.

I jerk my hand away, then touch the slab again, this time holding my hand steady. I step away, shaking with angst.

"We shouldn't do this today," I whisper, then repeat it louder.

The King is Born

But no one hears me as Thales has just joined us, hobbling on crutches. As soon as he sees me, he waves a crutch in my direction.

"Come on, Basilikos! You go first! You're the heir apparent. Show us how it's done. Be our fearless leader!"

"It's too dangerous! We can't do this today!"

"Coward!"

"You're so brave and strong and-" My fear turns to anger. It would serve him right! "You go first!"

"You know I can't with my leg you broke!"

"I'll go!" Demetres pushes past me.

"No! Don't!" I grab Demetres' arm and see a flash of water over his face. "You mustn't go down there! You'll drown!"

Demetres pauses, looking back at me. The others start calling him names.

"Listen to him, Demetres!" Gaius tries to stop him, too. "You know he 'sees' things."

"Are you a coward, too, Demetres?" Demands Dinias, brave with the courage of the crowd. Demetres pulls away from me and jumps in the opening. The boys run along beside the aqueduct.

"Oh, Mighty One, creator of goodness and light, let him live." The words pound to the rhythm of my heart. "Please let what I saw not happen!"

The others laugh and pound on the stone coverings. They get to the city wall, and flop down on the top of the aqueduct, waiting for Demetres to shoot out and splash into the pool below.

And wait.

And wait.

"He's stuck somewhere!"

"Start pushing the stones off!"

"Go get a grown up!"

As the others try desperately to find Demetres, I stagger against the wall, slide to the ground, making myself as small as possible.

Angry, condemning male voices

Boys crying

Chapter Eight - A Premonition

Stone grating against stone

A shout!

Feet shuffling and water dripping.

Shadows passing.

Silence.

❦

That night I went to my father's study. As usual he was poring over a manuscript. I slipped into the room, stood close to his side, and drew comfort from his nearness.

"So, Basilikos," he said without looking up, "what happened today with Demetres?"

"I tried to tell him not to go."

"You've been told time and again not to play in the aqueducts!"

I hung my head. He put down the quill with which he had been making notes and turns to look at me, waiting for my response.

"I saw it."

"Tell me." His voice suddenly gentle.

"We were bored, and hot. Once the Master had fallen asleep as he usually does after the noon meal, we slipped out and went to the old part of the city. As soon as I touched the aqueduct, I saw someone drowning. I tried to tell them not to go, but Thales arrived and kept baiting me. Then Demetres said he'd go first and jumped up on the ledge."

"Did you just think that he might get caught?"

"No! I tell you!" I looked up into his eyes. Steady eyes. Understanding eyes. "I saw it!"

"How? When?"

"When he pushed me out of the way to go first."

"So, when he touched you, you saw what was going to happen." I nodded. "And you tried to stop him?" I nodded, the tears finally starting to fall. "Why didn't he stop?"

"The others laughed at him and called him names." I look into those eyes as deep blue as the desert sky. "He had to go," I plead.

THE KING IS BORN

He nods, then pulls me against his chest. I bury my face in his robe, sobbing out the release that had to come. He lifts me onto his lap and cradles me as he did when I was a baby, until I lie exhausted and quiet.

He speaks, but not to me. Mother's soft voice answers. He stands with me in his arms as if I am light as a feather and carries me up to the rooftop where we sleep in warm weather. He lays me on his own bed and settles beside me. Mother lies on my other side. I'm cocooned between them and instantly fall asleep.

Chapter Nine
Rachel's Story

⁓♥♥⁓

    Mother is soft-spoken and as gentle as a doe. Father confessed his undying love for her and refused to take more wives. He gave her a complete set of rooms, too, not as a bribe to convince her of his love, but because she was an only wife.

    Mother does not need to work, either, but she had a passion for creating tapestries in which she tells the history of both Father's people and her own. She also weaves fabric from which our clothing is fashioned. In the beginning, she used the wool from our camels, but as the influence of our tribe grew greater and traders from all parts of the known world stop there, she learned to clean, spin, and weave flax from Egypt and silk from China. The garments she creates are some of the finest I have ever seen.

    As I sit and watch her spinning or weaving, she tells me the stories of her people, and since Father had said it was important to learn her heritage as well as his, I listen eagerly.

    Her people were the Israelites who had been conquered and taken into captivity by the Babylonians. For several generations, they had been held captive, but when they had finally been freed to return home, my mother's own family had chosen to stay in Babylon and so had continued in captivity.

    I especially love the story of how my parents met. Silly and terribly romantic, but, to me, it is what true love must be like. I also love the little smile that curls the corners of her mouth when I ask her:

    "Mother, tell me how Father found you."

    "Oh, Basilikos, you've heard it a hundred times!" She always says, and that tiny smile curls her lips.

    "I know, but I love to hear it and you love to tell it."

The King is Born

"All right, if you insist" The sounds of the loom return as she continues. "I was only fourteen when your father first saw me. I was drawing water at the well for my master's sheep when I saw your grandfather's camel caravan coming up the road. I tried to hurry so that I'd be done and out of the way for them, but the sheep would not hurry. They were thirsty and wanted to drink their fill. The well was deep and the bucket heavy. I was struggling with it when an arm reached over my shoulder and grabbed the rope.

"Here, let me help you," said a rich deep voice in my own language. He grabbed the rope just below mine and pulled the bucket up effortlessly. I looked up into his face, so close to mine and looked into those blue eyes. I don't think I had ever seen anyone's eyes that closely before, let alone such blue ones. It was several moments before I realized my face was uncovered. I quickly pulled my veil over my face and thanked him. He finished watering the sheep for me and offered to help me take them home. But sheep don't like a stranger's voice and they began to scatter. I thanked him politely and asked him to just stand back and be quiet. I didn't dare look at him as I desperately tried to gather the sheep, but I was so flustered that my motions and the tone of my voice alarmed the sheep. It was some time before I could quiet myself and them. All the time I could see him just standing there with his hands on his hips watching me. I was never so glad to get away from anyone!

"I didn't think I would ever see him again. Why would I? He was a stranger and besides, he was obviously a nobleman, and I was only a slave. Then there he was the next day at the well. He greeted me and stepped aside so the sheep would not be frightened. He had already drawn water and filled the troughs for me. I didn't know what to say, so I simply said thank you and made sure the sheep all got water."

"And the next day he was there again, right?" I ask.

"Ummm. There he was. He was so handsome. Tall and thin, but I could tell he was well built even under his robes. I looked him over carefully this time, for I knew it was no accident that he was there. As he drew more water for the sheep, I studied his hands. They were well cared for, the fingers long and lean, the nails cut evenly. The backs of his hands were covered with fine golden hair and the veins showed as he gripped the rope. His arms were strong

Chapter Nine - Rachel's Story

and brown, as if he was not used to wearing long-sleeved robes but was able to do a day's work. As he leaned over the well, his robe fell open and I could see that his chest was brown, too. I had thought he was much younger, for he was clean-shaven, but now I saw the creases around his eyes and the shadow of a beard, and I realized that he must shave daily. I judged him then to be a mature man - at least in his late twenties." She smiled. "Remember, I was only fourteen. Thirty seemed very mature." She is silent for a minute as she leans back and studies the pattern she is making.

"I am going to have to pull this out. I've made a mistake." I look at what she has done.

"No, Mother, don't take it out. It's actually quite pretty."

"You are right. This will certainly be a different rug, won't it?"

"Who knows, maybe you will start a new fashion! Tell me more about you and Father."

"Let's see, he had been at the well for the third time."

"He began to talk to you then, didn't he?"

"Yes. He asked me to whom I belonged and if I was betrothed. I told him who my master was and that I was not betrothed but had been promised to my master's head servant. He must have heard the distaste in my voice.

"'You don't sound too happy about that. Is he a very old man?' He asked, as if it really didn't matter.

"'Yes,' I said. 'He's very old, at least forty.' He laughed.

"'Well, that is old! And beside he's nasty and dirty and drinks too much wine.'

"'What else?' When I hung my head and refused to say more, he made that harmuph-ing sound that I have grown to love so dearly.

"'What you are saying is that he's a lecherous, dirty old man.'

"'I didn't say that!' I cried, terrified that someone might hear, although there was no one anywhere near us. 'I didn't say that and I will deny it if you tell anyone!'

"'I won't say a word!' He said. I looked up at him. He was smiling, his blue eyes almost lost in the crinkles at the corners. "Good day, miss.' And he bowed and strode away.

The King is Born

"I was mortified. All afternoon I wondered what he had gone to do. What if he told my master, or his head servant? What would happen? At the least, I would get a beating for talking to a stranger - a man at that!

"That evening, my master called for me. I went in fear and trembling. I was so frightened that I could hardly stand. He'd beaten me before, so badly that I would have died but for the care of another servant.

"'You are to pack what belongings you have tonight,' he said without even looking at me. 'Tomorrow you will be given over to Madjid, son of Jenghiz. For some reason, Madjid's son has taken a fancy to you and Madjid has paid a handsome sum to release you from my ownership and from the contract to marry Ictinus.' He looked me up and down and continued: 'I do not see what he sees in you, but then the Israelite women have never appealed to me. Go! Go in peace!'

"The next day I joined the women in the caravan as it prepared to leave. The women looked me over with reservation but treated me well enough.

"When we arrived here, I was taken to Madjid's harem and bathed, scrubbed and oiled and fed all sorts of sweets and treats to fatten me up, as I was deemed too skinny. For two weeks this went on, until one day the routine was broken.

"They washed my hair and rubbed it dry with oils and perfumes and twisted it up on my head with flowered vines and placed precious jewels everywhere. They rubbed my whole body down with more oils and perfumes. They dipped the tips of my fingers and toes in henna and rubbed rouge on my lips. They darkened my eyelids with the tip of a burned stick. Then they brought clothes for me to put on. I'd never seen anything like them! Of course, you are used to seeing the clothes the brides wear, but I'd never seen anything like it! I had always worn loose robes with just a rope knotted around my waist. What they wanted me to put on was far more lavish than anything they were wearing. But no one would say a word. I refused to put on the clothes, pulling my own familiar robe more tightly around me, I ran to a corner and curled up in a tight ball. I cried and cried.

Chapter Nine - Rachel's Story

"Then, a gentle hand touched my shoulder, and a soft voice spoke to me. Loving arms drew me from the corner and pressed my head against her. It was Issaca and she held me as a mother holds a weeping child.

"'Rachel,' she said. 'No one has explained to you what is happening, have they?' I shook my head. 'You are going to marry my son, Balthazar tonight. These women have been told to prepare you for the wedding. I said it was too quick, but he insisted. He's agonized over you ever since he first saw you at the well.'

"I looked up into her face, realizing for the first time what had happened.

"'I thought I had been bought as a slave,' I whispered. 'The man at the well that helped me water the sheep?' She nodded. 'Oh!'

"'You are not pleased with this?'

"'Oh! Oh, yes! He isn't nearly as old as Ictinus and much better looking.' She laughed and I looked up at her in fear of having insulted her.

"'It's quite all right, my child,' she said stopping the gush of words of apology. 'I know exactly what you mean. I understand that this Ictinus was a rather nasty, lecherous old man. I believe your fate with my son will be much better. He's young and healthy and very much in love with you. Now, you are obviously in no condition to be married today. I will go and tell my son he will have to wait a week for you. No! I insist! Any woman should have at least a week to prepare for her marriage! You have much to learn of our customs. He simply cannot expect - or demand any less!' And with that she stood up and drew me to my feet and led me to her own quarters.

"Oh, what a week that was! I had so much to learn!"

"What did she teach you, Mother? You've never told me."

"That is because it is women's business that you need to know now."

"That's what you always say!" I protest. She usually changes the subject. She put down her shuttle and studied me.

"How old are you Basilikos?"

"I'm fifteen, Mother. Surely you know that!"

"Yes," she says with a faraway look in her eyes. "They've

THE KING IS BORN

prepared you well for your future as Magus and Ruler, but have they prepared you to be a good husband?"

"Pah!" I said getting up and swaggering to the window as my father might do, hands clasped behind my back.

"What's there to it? No one has to tell me how to be a good husband."

She doesn't respond, so I turn back to her.

"Really, Mother! I know how other men treat their wives, but I know, also, how Father treats you. I wouldn't dream of treating my wife – or wives – any different."

She continues to study me across the room.

"What?" I demand.

"I wonder."

"About what?"

"Will you take a wife?"

"Why? Because of the Power?" When she says nothing, I throw out my arms like one of Grandfather's more theatrical gestures. "I already know and do just about all it can teach me."

"Be careful, Basilikos!" Mother's voice is suddenly sharp. "The Power is a jealous lover. It demands to be first. Do not put yourself before it!"

"Father said something like that." The bluster is as suddenly gone from me. "Do you think I'm putting myself first?"

"I think it's just bravado. I think, when the time comes, you will know what you must do. Yes. You have chosen to be Magus, but you are also the only heir to take on the role of Clan Leader."

"I know that. I shall also rule as Father does."

"Madjid rules this tribe, Basilikos." Her voice is once more sharp and I find myself resenting her as she continues. "It would be good to remember that!"

"Grandfather?" I feel the need to assert my own knowledge and strength. I am less than respectful to him - or her. "He's an old man! He's a figurehead. You don't attend the council meetings, Mother. You don't see it!" I miss the smile that curves Mother's lips, too busy on being self-important.

Chapter Nine - Rachel's Story

"He blusters and rants and throws temper tantrums until everyone is shaking in their sandals. Father has to settle him down and bring order to the meeting. It is he that makes the decisions!"

"Everything is not always as it seems, Basilikos," she warns, gently, which irritates me all the more.

"Mother!" I turn from the window and walk to the door. I've had enough of this conversation. "You don't understand these things. How could you? You're only a woman!" I shut the door none too quietly as I leave.

Chapter Ten
Calling the Fire

⁘

During the winter months Issaca also welcomes me into her rooms as a student. Issaca – I seldom called her Grandmother anymore – was the first wife of Grandfather Madjid. She could only give him one son, my father, Balthazar. Grandfather's tribe needed building up, so, even though he swore Issaca was his true love, he took many more wives who gave him many more sons.

To prove his favor for Issaca, he allowed her to have a complete set of rooms all to herself, close to his. It creates dissension among the women in his harem, but that doesn't seem to matter. In fact, I think Grandfather Madjid rather enjoys it!

Issaca is eccentric. She is fluent in several languages and full of lore, always eager to learn more about other peoples, their legends, customs and religions. Some whisper that she is a witch, even a Druid – a very secret cult that worships the moon and are purported to practice human sacrifices. The druids live in the dark reaches of a country called Gaul of which little is known.

I love Issaca and her rooms. I've never questioned her skills, nor the fact that she is only a woman, but readily absorb all she can teach me about the herbs she collects during the hot months, the salves and potions she makes - even poisons - and the uses for them. She has taught me about the human body, how it is believed to function; how to stop bleeding; how to cleanse a wound; even to cut away the poisoned flesh and draw the edges together with a needle and sinew made from the lining of the sheep's stomach. And as I've already shared, I watched her set Thales leg. And later, when one of the servants broke his leg, she called me to watch how she set it, wrapping the leg tightly between two short poles so that it would heal straight again.

⁘

The King is Born

And it was during this time that she taught me how to call the fire.

It is one of the easiest tricks, therefore one of the first to learn, and probably one of the last to lose. But fire, real or conjured, can burn out of control, and destroy everything in its path.

The leather curtains at the windows and over the door are drawn tightly against a howling wind that blows snow horizontally. A huge fire crackles in the massive fireplace. Braziers have been placed around the room, the flames dancing with the drafts. Issaca and my mother, Rachel, are working on their tapestries, their looms drawn close to the warmth of the fireplace. Other women spin wool, or stitch on clothing. I'm lying on the floor, tracing the patterns on the rug that my grandmother made.

A log shifts in the fireplace and one of the women replenishes the fire and the braziers. The brazier closest to me sputters and threatens to go out. I focus on it, my thoughts on how nice it is to have a roaring fire, when, suddenly, fire leaps, licking the kindling, sputters, then rises in steady flames.

"Did you do that, Basilikos?" Issaca.

"Do what?" I continue to stare at the fire.

"Did you bring the fire?" I look at her then.

"How could I do that?"

She tells one of the women to bring a clean brazier, set it in the center of the room and lay fresh fuel in it. Then she sits close to me.

"Keep your eyes on the brazier," she says. "Empty your mind of all thoughts."

That's not easy now, questions dance through my head: How? Why?

"See the shadows leap on the wall. Imagine the flames flickering over the wood."

The silence in the room is broken only by the crackle of the fires and the howling of the wind. I do as she bids me, seeing the leaping shadows on the walls.

"Call the fire." Her voice is soft, a whisper in my ear.

I call to the fire.

Chapter Ten - Calling The Fire

A whiff of smoke, a flame flickers, subsides. Fire explodes, roaring ceiling-ward, licks down the legs of the brazier.

"Close your eyes!" Issaca.

With an effort, I close my eyes. The flames subside to a gentle dance.

"You will learn in time to control the fire." She pats my shoulder.

Now I often call the fire, learning to bring it when I want it, letting it come gently, or in roaring flames. It's fun on those long winter days to play with fire. I can make the flames leap and dance, creating fanciful shadow-scenes on the walls. The cheery crackle also keeps at bay the terrible sound of the rain outside.

I hate the rain, the heavy winter rain that falls in thick sheets across the land.

I hate it because of the recurring dream:

Rain. Rain. Rain.

Sheet after sheet, marching down the mountains.

No wind. No thunder. No lighting.

Just rain.

Water is everywhere: seeping from under the aqueduct coverings; overflowing the lake's shores and fountain basins; turning the courtyards into lakes, the allies and streets into rivers.

Water gushing

Roaring

Ripping

Tearing

Chaos

Destruction

Death

Yes, the fire's preferable to the rain, but there are times when the fire gets away from me, threatening to consume me.

I am afraid of the fire, too.

Chapter Eleven
Basil Receives Ruby

෬♥༼෬

The Rite of Passage came in late Autumn, but it left no profound impact on me. The pain of the circumcision seemed as nothing compared to the pain of the loss of Demetres.

Now we were considered to be men. We put off the robes of youth and donned instead the robes of our calling. I had a choice: the purple robe of royalty or the blue robe of the Magi. I chose the blue.

෬♥༼෬

"Basilikos, my Lord," The servant bows to the room. A brazier stands in the middle of the floor, the flames guttering in the draft from the open door, creating shadows that leap up the walls and deepen in the corners.

"Come in and shut the door." The beloved voice speaks from those shadows. I step forward and the servant shuts the door behind me. Pausing just inside, I take a deep breath, savoring the odors of dusty books and musty old manuscripts.

"You did well," he says. I nod. "You showed yourself to be a man."

I watch the flames in the brazier as they curl around the embers, flickering and dancing to an unheard tune. My whole body aches. My groin throbs. My penis burns as if it is on fire. No preparation for the Right of Passage could ever prepare you for the burning pain of the circumcision. And yet, the pain is welcome. It matches the pain of the loss of Demetres.

"Your Father has something he wishes to give you."

"Mother?" I look up, shaken from my thoughts. I shade my eyes from the flames to better see her.

"I asked your mother to be here. I wanted her to share this moment."

The King is Born

He lights an oil lamp that stands among the clutter on his desk, and in the warmth of its glow I can see them both clearly. His square jaw is clean-shaven, making him look younger. She is beautiful. Her auburn hair, loosed from the accustomed shawl, shimmers as if it had a life of its own.

"Well! Are you going to stand there all night?"

"Forgive me, Father, I was thinking." I square my shoulders, take a deep breath and move around the brazier to stand in front of the massive Mahogany desk.

"Manhood changes many things." He says, lounging back in his great chair. "You will pursue your learning and take your place in the leadership of this tribe, both as leader and as High Magus. You will take a wife – or wives – and continue the legacy of this tribe. Our times together will become rare."

Without looking at Mother, Father stretches his hand toward her.

"It is time." Mother places a velvet pouch in his open hand. I watch with fascination as he undoes the ties of the pouch.

"You have seen this before. Many times. You played with it as a child. And you know the story well." I smile as I realize he is talking about the gemstone that usually hangs around his neck on a heavy gold chain. Yes, I know the story well: the destruction of the first village and the death of the High Priest; the ruins and how Grandfather found them; the fouled lake with the gemstone lying hidden deep in the mud.

"Your grandmother wore it for many years," Father.

"I didn't know that!" I am surprised. "Why would she have it?"

"She is the one who found it."

"But I thought you did. You are the one who ordered the pool emptied. You dug out all the mud around the remains."

"I did, that is true," Father speaks reflectively. "But it was Issaca who was haunted by the vision. It was her passion that drove us to find the ruins.

"After we emptied the pool and found the bones of the high priest, our High Priest left us. Issaca became the High Priestess.

Chapter Eleven - Basil Receives Ruby

"When she retired, she gave me the stone. It's a beautiful thing," he added, tipping the pouch up, allowing its contents to drop into his palm.

As he flattens his hand, a flash of red blinds me.

Red dances in the flames of the brazier, images appearing and disappearing so quickly I can't make them out. Emotions - joy, laughter, sorrow. Humiliation, pain, agony. I drop to my knees as it becomes too much for me.

"Close your eyes!" Father demands.

I gasp and close my eyes tightly.

⁓♡♥⁓

When I finally open them, my vision steadies and I can see what he holds in his hand: the human-heart shaped ruby in its golden cage that I'd played with as a child.

Now it lies still, the firelight catching and glimmering in its many facets.

Mother takes it from him and comes around the desk to fasten the chain around my neck. The deep red jewel swings on its chain, then settles on my chest, shimmering and pulsing with each beat of my own heart.

"This ruby has a legacy," Mother speaks gently from beside me. "It has no special powers. It will not protect you. It will not guide you - "

"No special powers! Won't protect you! Won't guide you! What sort of legacy is that? Don't say it, Creator! I know I did not protect Xanthos."

A woman's voice. I look around the room, but no one else was with us.

"- But wear it in honor of the one who gave his life for his child." She kisses me on the forehead.

"Who is speaking? " I search the shadows of the room.

"OH! He heard me, Creator!" Excitement.

"I was explaining to you about this pendant." Mother.

I shake my head. "No someone else - a woman."

"You heard a voice?" Father sounds excited.

49

The King is Born

"What?" I'm confused!

"Just now. You said that you heard a voice. No one else is here with us."

"I did. I heard a woman's voice object to Mother's statement about powers and protection. It mentioned Xanthos. Who is he?" I walk to the brazier, turning the caged ruby this way and that, watching the firelight's reflections.

"When you handed ... this to me I raise the ruby. "It flashed red. Like fire. Like fresh blood flowing. It spilled over everything, filling the room." I pause and continue in a whisper. "It flowed into me." The words seem to echo in the sigh of the coals in the brazier and the rustle of the window leather.

I hear the scrape of his chair as Father comes around the desk, not to me, but Mother. Although my back is turned to them, I see them as plainly as if they stood before me. Mother looks up at him, a question in her eyes. He tightens his arm, stilling her against his side.

"There was more, wasn't there." It's a statement.

"Yes," Trying to keep the vision of my parents before me, but the memories of the recent specters demanded my attention.

"Glimpses. Impressions." I shiver. "Voices. Raucous laughter. Shouting. Weeping. Agony. Intense agony." I shake my head trying to dispel the memory, but it persists.

Father tightens his arm around Mother's waist. They wait in silence.

"What does it mean, Father?" As I swipe my eyes on my sleeve.

"I believe it was the vision that Issaca and I have seen: The destruction of the village that once stood here. The death of the Leader and the abduction of the child." His voice is deep with emotion.

"I've seen those visions before when I played with the necklace as a child. I know Xanthos' end.

But I saw the face of a sweet, laughing child. Was he the kidnapped child?" I shake my head and study the ruby.

Chapter Eleven - Basil Receives Ruby

"It can't be! It felt like he is of the future as was the man hanging on a cross, blood and water flowing from his side. I felt his agony. Who is he?"

"Oh, my son!" Father releases Mother as she cries out, but it is he who crosses to me, lifting me to my feet and wrapping his arms around me, holding me tightly against his chest. After a moment, he speaks into the top of my head.

"You have seen more than either Issaca or me. I believe you have seen into the future. In time, we will know what this means. Somehow it is connected. Somehow it will all make sense, one day. We will know in time, my son. It is always revealed, in time"

"There's that word Time again!" That woman's voice again. I ignore her.

I manage a grin. " I just hope it doesn't take another five hundred years to find out! "

༺♡༻

Later that evening I return to my rooms. I don't bother to light a candle as there's a full moon shining through my window. I push my bed under the window and undo the chain with the ruby on it.

"When Mother put this gemstone around my neck, I heard a female voice. There was only Father and Mother in the room with me. So, I want to know whose voice I heard!"

Silence.

"Look! I've heard voices before! Grandmother Issaca and I have communicated by thought when we weren't together. And I've seen visions!" I shake my head. "Don't want to talk about those!"

I study the ruby, turning it this way and that.

"Grandmother says it's natural for us - her and me - 'cause we're different from others. So. Who are you? Where are you? And why can I hear your voice?"

"I'm sitting in your hand at the moment."

"No way!" I drop the ruby as I jump off the bed. The ruby sparkles in the moonlight and I hear a woman's laughter. I prowl the room.

The King is Born

"I don't know that expression yet. Issaca is the only one who has ever talked to me. Everyone else ignores me. Even the visions I show them."

I stop pacing. "Visions? What visions?"

"Warnings, usually. Things that are going to or could happen. Whatever Creator tells me to show."

I pick up the ruby. The moonlight sparkles in its facets and a beam of light flashes out of it onto the wall. I follow the light and almost drop the ruby again, for in the light beam is a woman with long auburn hair showing under a shawl. Thoughtful gray-green eyes watch me in return.

"I see a woman!"

"It's me, Ruby. I've discovered humans are less frightened if they can see me."

"Was it you that showed Grandmother the visions of where you were hidden?"

"No, I was not able to communicate while I was stuck in the mud. But before that I did try to warn Xanthos of the coming danger. He didn't understand, to his demise."

"He was the leader of the tribe that first settled here. He was killed and his baby son was kidnapped. Right?"

"Yes."

"What happened to the baby? Did he live?"

"Yes, he lived and still lives. You will meet him one day. But now you must rest. You have had a harrowing day. Good night."

The image disappears. I pick up the gem in its cage and settle on my bed, trying to still my racing thoughts.

Chapter Twelve
Discussions

I've spent more and more time with my father, learning all he can teach me and sharing with him what I learn from the monks I meet on my journeys through the Hindu Kush. He is an avid scholar, his thirst for knowledge leading him down many avenues and I follow close behind him.

He continues to teach me the functions of the Magi and, because I will also be the ruler of our people, he allows me to sit in on the council meetings. Afterwards, he questions me about what I saw and heard and perceived. He's teaching me how to read people by their stance, their expressions, gestures. It comes easily, as did the "sight."

Now I am beginning to understand how my father and grandfather work in the council meetings. Remembering Mother's words that everything is not always as it seems, I'm paying better attention today. It fascinates me to see the difference between the two men and how they perceive and react to different situations. Father is quiet, respectful, almost gentle. Grandfather is a fiery old man, full of huff and puff, theatrical in all his dealings, manipulative and cunning.

I've never cared to spend much time with Grandfather as he frightens me.

He is a big man. Big in every way.

He's taller than my father and possibly as robust as he is tall. The robes he wears, even in the hot summer, are voluminous, fold upon fold of fabric. When he gets in one of his rages, he swirls those robes as he stomps up and down the Hall until he seems twice as big as normal.

And his voice! It's deep and comes all the way from his toes. In anger, it booms through the whole palace.

The King is Born

His laugh is almost as frightening as his voice. It rumbles around in his belly - you can see it - and then it gurgles up through his throat until it bursts out of his mouth with such vigor that it makes the lamps shudder.

Even in his quiet moments, he is big.

⁑

On one of those rare occasions when we found our paths to wander side by side for a while, I asked him about his relationship with his son. It was on a particularly sweltering hot summer afternoon when we had strolled out to sit in the cool of the long grass under the orange trees in the orchard.

"Grandfather," I began. "Will you promise not to get upset with me if I ask you a question?" The old man chuckles.

"How could I possibly get upset with you, my favorite grandson?"

"It's about you and Father. I have been watching you when you meet with the elders. You are very different in the way you handle things."

"Yes, we are," he says, the amusement still in his voice. "It works well, doesn't it?"

"What does?"

"Oh, I know what people say about me. I am a fiery old tyrant who throws temper tantrums at will. I do a good job of scaring everyone. Just at the right moment, Balthazar steps forward and, with his gentle ways and calm voice, settles me down, soothes their ruffled feathers and there you have it. They never knew what got them." He chuckles again. I stared at him open mouthed.

"It's all an act, young Basilikos, don't you understand? Watch closely and you will see that your father is very cunning, calculating and just as manipulative as I am. Under his gentle ways is a man carved of granite. He doesn't budge an inch and he always, I mean always, gets what he wants.

"Your father is a great man, Basilikos. Every day I thank my lucky stars that the Mighty One saw fit to bless me with such a son and my first-born, at that!" Silence follows for a bit.

Chapter Twelve - Discussions

"I admire your father for refusing to take another wife, you know. I wish I'd been so strong. But, when we first established this city, the tribe desperately needed building up."

I keep still. When Grandfather begins to ramble, you never know where it will lead.

"I love your grandmother. Almost as much as your father loves your mother. And just like your mother, she was unable to bear any more children after the first baby. But. I gave in to the pressures and took more wives. It broke her heart. The other women lorded it over her. I try hard to make her feel better by telling her how much I love her. I always bring her home the most beautiful silks and jewelry and perfumes and ointments. I always spend the first night back with her. But I've a responsibility to my other wives and to the tribe and until the day she dies, the fact that I must produce children without her will be a great sorrow to her. Some women are like that."

"I don't think I'll ever get married," I lie back in the grass and look up into the bows of the orange tree.

"Why do you say that?"

"Well, I just feel it here," I dig my fingers into the pit of my stomach. "Besides, girls don't seem to interest me like they do the other boys."

"You are not a boy anymore, Basilikos. You are a young man. And soon you will have to accept the responsibilities facing you. After your father, you are the next in line as leader of this great tribe. It is your responsibility to marry many women and produce many sons."

"Yes, but I just don't have any interest in them!"

"That is beside the point!" Gruffly. "You will marry, and you will sire sons. What you do other than that is up to you. But it is better not spoken of in our social circles. There are many men like you, the gods know. Too many by far. Now! Leave me. I wish to be alone to think."

I jump up and run, afraid of the rage that has come over him.

For several days, I ponder over that conversation. I don't understand what Grandfather had been talking about, or what had made him so upset. Ruby's no help, either. It's a mystery to her, too.

The King is Born

This evening Father and I are working together over some new manuscripts that he had just purchased.

He stops, carefully putting down his pen, and sits back in his chair.

"Do you want to talk about it?"

"Talk about what?"

"You are not concentrating on the task at hand," he says. "You keep staring into the flame of the lamp and sighing great big sighs. What can possibly be bothering you? Are you in love?"

"Love! Oh, that's rich!" I get up and go to the window, staring at the landscape in the light of the moon, as if, perhaps, I could find an answer there. I speak without turning around.

"A few days ago, Grandfather and I had a chance to talk."

"That's good. You need to be with him more. He feels you are ignoring him."

"Ignoring him? No! More likely avoiding him! He frightens me! I don't understand him and now I've managed to upset him. I don't know what I said or did."

"Tell me what happened." He speaks quietly and I know that if I could manage to look into his eyes, they would be that deep desert-sky blue. But I cannot. I relate what happened without turning from the window.

"What did I say wrong, Father?"

"You said nothing wrong, Basilikos. It was the assumption Grandfather made that was wrong. Tell me, what do you mean when you say you have no interest in women?"

"Well, the other boys - young men, as Grandfather would remind me - talk incessantly about women. What they look like. What they do. Some of them have already slept with some of the servant girls and have shared, in detail, the experience. The other fellows get very excited over the descriptions. Then they start bragging about what they've done, or what they would have done in the same situation. I find it rather embarrassing. No, more than that. I guess, because of the love I have seen you show toward Mother, I cannot imagine doing what they talk about doing to someone I love."

Chapter Twelve - Discussions

"There's the catch, Basilikos. What they're doing is not out of love, but out of lust, a desire for power over others. Power over the women as they take them and power over the other boys as they share what they've done, trying to outdo each other to prove they're more powerful."

"It's not like I'm not attracted to women," after a moment or two. "I am. I find them fascinating. They are so mysterious with their veiled faces and bodies covered from head to foot with layers of fabrics. I mean, I've seen Mother and Grandmother Issaca without their veils on and only their house robes. But they're older. I mean," I hastened to rephrase my words as my father chuckles.

"I know what you mean, but for heaven's sake don't let either of them hear you say that!"

"Of course not! I'm not that stupid! I'm not!" I protest at the expression on his face.

"Go on. You were talking about mysterious women."

"Haven't you ever wondered what they look like under all those layers? What do they feel like? The other boys talk about skin smoother than silk and breasts soft as downy pillows. And then they talk about doing "it". What's "it" like? Is it really as they say?"

"I can well imagine what they tell you, Basilikos. But let me tell you this: Man is made to procreate. It's in our loins. It's in our blood. For some men, it's in their head and that's all they think about. They relate everything they do to the sexual act - or to battle - and sometimes they get the two mixed up."

"Yah! From some of the things they say it sounds like it's a battle! How can a person treat another person like that?"

"In our society, women are seldom thought of as anything more than chattel - put on earth for man's pleasure. They are not people; they are objects to use and abuse and discard at will."

"That is not how you feel about Mother, is it."

"No. I love Rachel. From the moment I first looked into her eyes, I have loved her. And I'll always love her. And respect her. Not many women would put up with a man that cannot and will not make love to them."

"What?" I stop to look at him.

THE KING IS BORN

"That's right. We made love once. And from that union you were conceived. I have never made love to your mother again."

"Why not? I mean, surely. They say once you've done it, you want it over and over again, that it is a hunger that consumes you."

"True."

"But not for you?"

"For me."

"Then why? Oh, because Mother had such a hard time giving birth?"

"No. That is a story your mother concocted to explain why she never had any more children. She could have and still longs for them."

"You're killing me, Father! Tell me, please!"

"The Power." He says it simply. He drops his hands, letting them dangle over the arms of his chair. He stares into the flame of the oil lamp on the desk and his voice goes soft, so soft I have to strain to catch all the words. "The Power demands it of you. It is all consuming. It will burn you in the end." A long silence follows as he watches the flickering flame. He turns his head to study me. Our eyes meet and hold for a long moment. "You will have to make the choice, Basilikos. I gave it up for the love of a woman. And I never fully recovered it, even though I have been celibate ever since."

"I don't understand. What choice?"

"The choice between the Power and a woman. The Power is a jealous lover, it demands absolute fidelity. It must be first and last and everything in between. It will not allow another being or object to come before it." He pauses again. "As you said, once you have known a woman, all your forces within you strive to know her again. And the more you know her, the more you want to know her. The lust for a woman becomes a never-ending passion. But. You cannot have both."

"But. You have the Sight, and you read the stars and you can perform magic."

"Tricks, Basilikos. Mere tricks. Anyone can read the stars with practice. The magic I do is sleight of hand, or simply knowledge not known by others. Yes, I have the Sight to a certain extent."

Chapter Twelve - Discussions

"But the way you "read" people."

"Practice. Oh, yes, perhaps it is a little more than that. There is intuition. A knowing that is unexplained. You have already experienced that. But already you have gone further than I have. You have the fire at your command. You have the Sight. You can read the thoughts of others. You dream dreams and see visions. You know the future. You are a prophet. You have the makings of a true Magus. The question is, will you be able to live up to the demand of the Power?"

There is no answer to that question. Only time will tell. We return to translating the manuscripts until I realize he had not answered my original question.

"Father, you never explained to me what Grandfather was so upset about."

"No. I didn't. Don't worry about it now. I'll set him straight."

"Does he know? I mean about you and Mother?"

"No."

"How will he understand?"

"Grandfather is not . . . without understanding. I will explain it to him. Now, it's getting late. You should be off to your bed."

I put away the manuscript and clean my pens, my mind full of questions.

Chapter Thirteen
The Invisible Cave

❧❧❧

Several years have passed, a rich tapestry of learning and training, of growing in the skills of the warrior, and in the challenges of the Council. With the girls safely ensconced in the harems preparing themselves for their betrothals, the boys have had no excuse but to work hard at their training.

I must confess that I have excelled in most areas. My eyes are keen with the bow and my aim true with the javelin. My body has eventually caught up with the other boys and, although I've never developed the muscular build of Dinias and Thales, my body is sinewy and strong. Because I'm not encumbered with their weight, I can out-run and out jump them and out-maneuver them in wrestling matches, but once they catch me, they pin me to the wall or floor with their superior weight and strength. They are boorish, big brutes with little intelligence. Consequently, I choose not to associate with them, but rather with Nicias and Gaius whose quick minds match and even challenge mine.

We often slip out into the mountains, sometimes riding for days. Gaius, at least, is tolerant of my desire to stop and examine every new plant we encounter. He helps me dig them up and carry it back to show Issaca. Nicias, more the man of action, waits and watches with amusement boarding on exasperation. He much prefers to chase down the wild game and is proud to carry back trophies of our hunt. Together we explore into the Hindu Kush as far as the snow line. We venture to the south, over the mountains and down into the valleys of Gandara and Arachosia. We explore to the north into Sogdiana. We keep to the mountains where the soaring cliffs and the magnificent vistas hold us in awe, but the Oxus Basin and the Great Deserts with rolling hills of sand never beckon to us.

❧❧❧

The King is Born

It's the day of the summer solstice of my seventeenth year, we are riding in the hills of Gandara. To the south, dark storm clouds threaten to topple over the southern mountains.

Gaius glances over his should as thunder rumbles and dust devils dance across the dry wash and the clouds tumble over the ridge and into the valley.

"Storms coming!"

"It's moving fast, too!" Nicias as we pull our horses to a stop.

"It's getting pretty late, and this storm will break at any moment," Gaius holds his horse in as a gust of wind whips the trees around us.

I study the cliff to the northeast and point, shouting as I spur my horse in that direction

The storm chases us as we race across the valley, lighting striking the ground where we had just been.

"Where are we going, Basil? There's no shelter here!" Gaius.

I search the cliff.

"Ruby are you sure there's shelter here?" I ask, telepathically.

"Look closer!" And as she says it, I see a cave mouth open in the cliff. I point to it and head in that direction, the others close behind. Lighting continues to strike around us, the last one striking above the cave's entrance as we enter. Rocks and debris rain down around us.

We dismount, attempting to calm our horses.

"That was close!" Gaius.

"Almost as if it were chasing us!" Marvels Nicias, glancing at me. I see the stilled movement of his hand and smile. Even my closest friends still fear other gods.

Two priests appear out of the gloom. They bow and hold out their hands for the reigns of our horses. I feel a tug on my sleeve and turn to see another monk beckoning for us to follow him. He takes a flaming torch out of a wall bracket and leads us deeper into the cave, which becomes a tunnel. Several times openings appear on our left or right. We make so many turns that I lose my bearings.

Finally, I see light ahead and we emerge into what must be an old sinkhole. I stop in awe.

Chapter Thirteen - The Invisible Cave

The floor is lush with all sorts of flowering plants and trees I don't recognize. I want to explore, but the monk tugs at my sleeve and leads us to a colonnade. At the far end, he opens a door and steps aside for us to enter.

Not knowing what to expect, I square my shoulders and lift my chin, and in the most regal voice I could, I thank him as I step through the door and stop so abruptly that Nicias and Gaius, following closely, bump into me. I move forward just enough to let them step up beside me. I hear their gasps as they, too, are overawed by what they see:

A cavern that seems to have no ceiling or walls, except for one with arched window open to the mountain view beyond. A giant fire pit with a fire burning merrily in it draws my attention. Spread around it are rows of rugs and pillows.

The monk motions for us to descend a wide staircase and leads us to the rugs closest to the fire. He bows and disappears in another direction.

"This is not like any monastery that we've seen before," whispers Nicias. I shake my head. "What do you think?"

"We could hold the yearly tournaments in here!" Gaius whispers in response.

"People are coming, Basil!" Ruby's warning comes as I sense another presence with us, not a good presence.

"Someone's coming," I whisper as I step away from them, drawing my cape of a Magus around my shoulders. I stand with my arms folded over my chest, my legs apart. Nicias and Gaius step up on either side and slightly behind. Their hands drop to the hilts of their swords hidden under their capes.

Light filters through the darkness, growing brighter as a line of torches bob toward us, revealing the figures carrying them. They wear long linen robes and dark, coarse cloaks over their shoulders. Their heads are shaven. Without a word, they move to their places and stand facing the stairs down which we had come.

"Another presence is here!" Ruby. *"It's evil!"*

"I feel it, Ruby. It doesn't want us here, does it?"

"I don't think so. But another comes. It looks like a beast!"

The King is Born

I turn, expecting to see a man in finery befitting his station, but instead see a figure, about four feet tall, swamped in a brown hooded cloak. It hops down the steps and trots right passed, ignoring us. I remain facing the stairs, wondering what I should do. It's like being in a dream world where nothing is how you expect it to be.

Curiosity gets the better of me and I turn to see where the creature has gone. All the monks are now facing the opposite direction. The fire light and the smoking torches are blocking my vision, so I push my way through the monks to discover a raised dais with a magnificent throne, ornately carved from stone. Its backrest towers higher than an average man, its width could seat two, comfortably.

Monks help the little figure up onto the throne where it settles, its face still hidden under its hood.

I walk to the foot of the steps, Nicias and Gaius close at my sides.

"I'm glad I'm not alone, Ruby. You and Nicias and Gaius - I'm feeling the presence of an evil force more clearly."

"Only the Monks hold it back, Basil. It wants a body. A person who is his by rights."

The figure on the throne sits stock still. After a moment, it raises what looks like cloven hooves, pushing back the hood, revealing first a snout, then what appears to be horns curled against the sides of its head, hiding its ears.

"It looks like a ram's skull!" Gaius in a gasped whisper.

My gaze meets the eyes. Huge, black eyes, filling his face and my vision, penetrating my very being. There are no secrets hidden from those all-seeing eyes.

I drop my head; my arms fall to my sides. I'm suddenly kneeling. Gaius and Nicias drop to their knees, as well.

The Ram begins to speak, his voice an irritating continuous bleat. I force myself to listen. The bleating softens into a lilting, melodic rhythm. It's soothing, gentle, the syllables repetitive, hypnotic. I hear familiar syllables and realize he's attempting to say my name.

Chapter Thirteen - The Invisible Cave

"Bay-zil. Bay-zil-kos." I look up. He nods. Random words stand out: "Far... this ... day... You ...horses ... over mountains."

"Yes!" I exclaim. "I – we – have come from near Bactria, from the city of Madjid."

Silence. Had I spoken too fast? I start to speak but stop as the man beside him shakes his head.

"Mad – jid." The Ram pronounces it correctly. "Bac-ti-ra." He shakes his head and waves his hand in dismissal.

"You! Bay-zil-kos!" He points a cloven hoof at me. "You -" his eyes drop to my chest and hisses, beckoning me to approach. As I move up the steps, he stands on the throne. We are eye to eye; however, his attention is still on my chest. He beckons me closer, thrusting his hooves inside my robe, he grabs the gold chain, pulling Ruby out and into the firelight.

"Don't let him take me!" Ruby's panicked voice shouts in my head. She dangles on her chain, catching the flickering flames of the torches. The ram hisses again. He looks up into my eyes and holds my gaze for what seems an eternity. Then he lays Ruby against my robe and turns to the man beside him, speaking quickly. The man listens, glancing at me, nods, and hurries away.

The Ram sits on the arm of the throne and beckons to me to take the throne. I'm surprised, raising my eyebrows in question. He taps the chair.

"Sit! Sit! Sit" His words are sibilant, hissing as a serpent. I shudder. Is this the evil I felt so strongly just before he appeared?

I sit and glance down at Nicias and Gaius. They stand, hesitant, at the bottom of the steps. I nod to them, and they take their places next to me.

It pays them no mind, its eyes once more intent on Ruby. He points to her.

"Where get?"

"Issaca -" he hisses and jerks back, his eyes narrow as they turn back to my face.

"How know Issaca?"

"My grandmother," hesitantly. He shakes his head. "My Father's mother." No response while he ponders my words.

The King is Born

"Yis! Yis! Yis!" Excited. "Grand moth – ir -r! Iss-ca! Yis!" He hops down off the arm of the throne and the dais steps, heading for the archway the men had entered earlier.

"Bay-zil-kos! Yis! Come!" I glance at Nicias and Gaius.

"Guess we follow Ramskull?" Nicias. I shrug. We head after the disappearing figure.

The little figure scurries along a tunnel, a monk ahead of him with a lighted torch. He never looks back to see if we have followed. Finally, he stops outside a door. The monk opens it for us.

"DANGER!" Cries Ruby as I step through the doorway into a bed chamber, large by normal standards. I stop just inside the door, gasping for breath, and recognize the evil I'd felt earlier.

"Death is here!" Ruby exclaims unnecessarily as his stench swirls through the dust. The stamping of hooves reverberates through the cave. In the far shadows, I glimpse a huge white Brahma bull with massive horns, blood oozing from a slit throat. Beside him, a black cape swirls.

I turn from the vision and see, through the murky light a dais with a large bed in disarray. A human figure moves restlessly under a blood-soaked cover.

I leap over the steps and pull the cover back. I'm not ready for what I see.

"You fix, Bay-zil-kos!" Ramskull demands. "You Iss-ca granson. You fix!"

I haven't recovered from the shock yet. Vaguely I realize that Issaca's fame as a medicine woman has reached here! And because I admitted to being her grandson, I am expected to do as she would.

"But how on earth am I going to do that? The man's been gored by a bull!"

The room blurs and dust swirls. Hooves clatter on stone. I assume it's the vision I'd first seen as I entered, returning. The ground shakes and something brushes my arm, ripping my sleeve. The huge beast roars past me, stamping and snorting.

The injured man whimpers, "The bull! The bull!"

I gasp, turning and spreading my arms wide to protect the man.

Chapter Thirteen - The Invisible Cave

"What bull, Basil?" Gaius sounds confused. I peer into the shadows. All is still. I check my sleeve. It's in one piece. I hear an evil laugh.

"He's mine, Basilikos. I will have him!"

"Not while I'm here, you won't!"

I turn my back to the shadows, ignoring the look exchanged by my cousins, and focus on the man in the bed.

Here is the cause of the foul odor in the room. His abdomen has been ripped open, his bowls torn, oozing blood and gore. The whole area is inflamed, pockets of puss have formed, broken and oozing, too.

"Nicias, I am going to need lots of hot water and loads of clean rags. Gaius, get the fire stoked. I want it to be blazing hot and very bright. Lots of light, too! I am going to find the kitchens and see what I can put together for him."

I turn to Ramskull, cupping my hands as if I held a bowl and began ladling food into my mouth. He gives instructions to his man to bring me food.

"No! No! No!" I exclaim. "I need to go to the kitchens! How do I make you understand!" I throw up my hands.

"Oshana" Ruby suggests. I repeat it, and immediately one of the monks motions me to follow him.

The kitchens are vast. Three huge roasting pits fill one end. Cauldrons bubble on hearths that are lined with baking ovens. Kettles and containers are stacked against another wall. Platters and jugs line carved out shelves on another wall. Long tables run down the center of the room covered with vegetables and game in all stages of preparation.

The aroma is delightful and inviting and reminds me I have not eaten since early this morning. A worker approaches. My guide explains my purpose. I hear Issaca's name and the man's eyes widen before he quickly bows to me and leads me to the cauldrons. In one, I find what I want – bird carcasses simmering. I sniff at it.

"What have you put in here?" He seems to understand, leading me to a table, with an assortment of ingredients.

"Issaca, can you hear me?"

The King is Born

"Basil! Yes. What's happening?"

"I need to make a healing broth, a wound cleaning solution and a drying powder. What do I need?"

"Onions, garlic. If nothing else, always onions and garlic!" Issaca responds.

There's a mound of them on the table. I add several onions and two heads of garlic to a pot and begin to examine the other things on the table, some of which I did not recognize. There's a whitish root with a very pungent odor.

"Gin-ger," the Worker.

What had Issaca told me about Ginger? "From India and China, it could be used internally and externally to reduce fever and inflammation."

Good! I add that to the pot, continue along the table, finding curious, long, dried, red pods. They have a hot smell

"Capsicum. Pep-per." The worker explains and waves his hand in front of his mouth as if he'd eaten something hot. I shake my head.

"Hot peppers are good for healing, but better used in a salve for healing flesh than eaten." Ruby adds. I put a bunch aside.

I added several other ingredients to the pot, then ladled the juice from the pot of fowl carcasses. The cook takes the pot from me and places it on a bed of coals, heaping them up around it.

While that cooks, I began to prepare the salve. Issaca suggests ingredients that would help the healing.

The worker touches my arm and points to a door. I follow him into a room that is light and airy. From its rafters, herbs, flowers and roots hang to dry.

"Now why didn't you show me this in the beginning!" I demand and clap him on the shoulder. He smiles at my obvious delight. I hurry down the rows smelling and examining the herbs. Lavender, hyssop, hemp, thyme, sage, and basil! I recognize these. I point to them and he pulls down bunches of each.

I hesitate when I come to the roots. The one I really want is not here.

Chapter Thirteen - The Invisible Cave

"Bistorta? Snakeroot?" I question the worker. He shakes his head. He has to have it! It's a staple in the mountains. The powdered root and is an antihermorragic, helping to stop bleeding and heal wounds. And I had seen it this very morning in the valley below, its pink tufts of flowers dancing in the breeze.

Suddenly I remember seeing those same flowers on the table in the other room. I return and grab them, pointing to where the root would have been. He nods and dashes back to the drying room and returns with the twisted root and a pouch of powder.

Now, armed with all the herbs, the poultice, and the pot of soup, we return to the sick room, which is brighter and cleaner, thanks to Nicias and Gaius. A fire dances in the hearth where a large cauldron full of water bubbles. Candles fill several candelabra around the bed.

"Good job, men! Perfect!"

They've also cleaned the bed and the man, both of which are draped with clean linens. Ramskull sits beside the bed, also dressed in a clean robe.

I glance around the room. As clean and fresh as it looks, I know: Death and the Beast are still here, lurking in the shadows, and, as if to confirm it, the beast stamps his hooves. I turn my back on the shadows and throw herbs into the fire and all over the floor, as Issaca has taught me to do.

The soup has cooled enough to be drinkable. Together, Nicias and Gaius help sit the patient up while Ramskull climbs on the bed and spoons soup into the eager mouth. When he refuses more soup, the men ready him for what will come next.

While we wait for him to drift off to sleep - for I had added opium to the soup - I have the men set up a long table and lay out my supplies on a small table beside it. As soon as the man is asleep, I have them move his body onto the table and, steeling myself, I examine the wound. The edges are caked with congealed blood, dirt, and straw. His guts protrude,

I have no idea how badly he is injured internally, neither have I the knowledge to help him there. I soak rags in the herbal tincture and squeeze the liquid into the wound, then lay the rags on the wound to soak it up.

The King is Born

I can hear the shuffling of the bull. The stench of death is thick, as thick as the shadows beyond the candlelight. I'm sweating, not only from the physical effort of cleaning the wound, but from the very real effort to keep fear at bay, because I know that if I give in to fear, Death will have his victim.

It's taking too long to clean the wound this way.

"Nicias, Gaius, help me roll him on his side and hold him there."

I sluice water into the wound, letting it run out onto the floor. All three of us vomit at the same time, but I keep sluicing the wound until finally it's cleaned out. We stop to let the monks clean up the floor and clean ourselves, too.

Returning to body, I dust all the raw edges with the powdered Bistorta root, sew up the intestines, adding more powder as I go. Finally, I take the last stitch and cut the thread, dust the whole area with a thick layer of powder and lay clean linen over it, Nicias and Gaius tie it in place. We move him back to the clean bed and I sit studying the face. It's gray and covered with a light sheen of sweat. His breathing is light, but even.

I stand, and, on inspiration pray aloud.

"Oh, One True God oversee his recovery."

A snort echoes from the shadows. Stinking air eddies around me. I settle on some cushions by the bed, ignoring the sounds and smells. Ramskull motions for me to go with him, but I shake my head. He mimes sleep and points to all three of us. Again, I shake my head again, pointing to my cousins.

"Nicias, Gaius, you get some sleep. I must stay with him."

They hesitate.

"Go! I will need you at your best tomorrow!"

"We can sleep here with you, Basil. You shouldn't be left alone."

"I won't be alone. Believe me!"

"Ramskull?" I shake my head. "You mean . . ." Nicias glances up. I nod. It's better he doesn't know what I face. "Well, all right, if you insist. We will just sleep for a little while and will return at first light."

Chapter Thirteen - The Invisible Cave

I nod, relieved that they will go. I must fight my own fears, I don't need theirs too.

They leave along with all but one monk and Ramskull. The room is quiet. I stoke the fire and set new candles in the candelabras.

Death makes his presence known, his voluminous black robes swirling with each movement, and with them, the shadows leap up the walls. The Beast's impatience increases as well, its stamping echoing in the crackle of the fire.

Ramskull settles on pillows to one side of the bed. The monk stays near the fire. I sit on the opposite side of the bed from Ramskull where I can watch my patient.

Through the night the we take turns replenishing the fire and the candles to keep light and warmth at its maximum. Twice I coax more broth into the man and change the poultice. The fever rages, and so does he. We hold him and bath him with the herbal water. I dip a mug into the cauldron of herbal water and encourage him to drink that, too.

Sometime in the wee hours of the night, in what is called the "Death Watch", I wake with a jerk. The candles have guttered low, and the fire is little more than embers. The monk is asleep by the fire. Ramskull is absent.

Death fills the room, the oppression so intense I can hardly breath. Gasping, I jump to my feet

"Get back!" I yell. "Death, you will not have this life tonight!" A roar fills the room, and a wind blows out the last of the candles.

"I will have him, Basilikos!" Death growls. "He is mine now!"

"No! I tell you! By the One True God! You will not take him!" I jump on the bed and straddle the body.

"*Ha! Ha! Ha!*" Howls Death, swirling his cloak around him.

The bull stamps its hooves and snorts.

"*You do not even know the name of this . . . god you call upon! What makes you think I am not he!*"

"The One True God is Light!" I yell and fling out my arm. Fire roars in the hearth. A response flashes from Ruby, as dislodged by my actions, she flies free of my tunic.

"*Use me, Basil!*" She cries.

The King is Born

I grab her and turn to the candles, aiming the shafts of light radiating from her, almost melting them attempting to light them faster than Death can blow them out.

The man beneath me moans, then begins thrashing. I lose my footing and fall, tumbling off the bed. Ruby flies from my hand as I hit the floor.

"I need help!" I gasp, scrabbling for Ruby. "Oh, Most High God! Send me help!"

Lightning flashes, a white, searing light. Thunder shakes the rock under me.

Only inches from my fingers, Ruby catches the light in her facets, sending blood-red rays crashing back into the room. They smash back and forth against the walls and roof, then coalesce over the restless body, moving its length and back again, settling over the wounded abdomen. The body stills. The man slips into a deep sleep.

The luminescence spreads, filling the room. I lift my head and sniff. Cool, clean air swirls around me, and I smile.

Death, and the Beast have left the cave.

୬୭୧୶

In the peaceful silence that follows, I fall asleep not to wake until the sibilant sound of excited voices trying to whisper, rouses me. I sit up and look around. The monk sits in front of a gentle fire, his head bent close to that of another monk I'd not seen before.

The patient still sleeps, his face and hair dry, his cheeks cool to the touch. Gingerly I draw back the covers and lift the dressing, and gasp in surprise.

"How is he?" Whispers Nicias as he and Gaius stop beside me.

"Um. Ah. See for yourself!" I move so they can see the body on the bed. Nicias swears, Gaius shouts something unintelligible. The monks hurry over and examine the patient's abdomen, muttering to each other.

They turn to me. The new monk is taller than me with black, searching eyes and a halo of white hair around his ears. A white goatee dresses his chin. His skin is bronzed and weathered with age. He grins, his eyes disappearing in wrinkles.

I gasp as I recognize him.

Chapter Thirteen - The Invisible Cave

"Ba-zil-kos!" His voice is normal - without the bleating!

"What's happened?"

He laughs. "Not only have you healed my son, you have broken the curse! You are truly a god!" And he begins to bow to me.

"No! No! No!" I cry. "I cannot take the credit."

Other monks are now filling the room. When they see Ramskull looking like a real man, they gather round and pat him and cry out in what is obviously great joy. He points to the bed and to me. The monks surround the bed, exclaiming with joy, then turn and begin bowing to me.

I threw my hands in the air. "Nicias! Gaius! Stop them!"

"Well, Basilikos," laughter in Gaius' voice. "Who can blame them? This is pretty miraculous! I would not have given a day's ration of bread for his life last night. And now here he is – awake!" I turn to see the fellow's eyes open, watching me.

"Hello!" I say.

Ramskull speaks to my patient in excited tones. My patient looks at me with wonder in his eyes, then says something to the monks and they carry me away.

෴

I'm finally re-united with Gaius and Nicias. I have been bathed and rubbed down with spiced oils and clothed in fresh royal blue and purple linen, clasped at the shoulder with a fine, filigree broach. Ruby sits proudly visible on my chest.

We are led back to the massive chamber in which we had first met Ramskull. The large cushions and pillows are now arranged around low tables that groan with loaves of bread, bowls of fruit, roasted mutton and sundry other delicacies. My patient sits on the throne, Ramskull beside him. When they see us approaching, they motion us to join them on the dais. We are ushered to a table set on the man's right side.

"This fellow you saved must be their ruler!" Gaius whispers.

"That would seem to be," I respond.

Answers don't seem to be coming, so we happily enjoy the food and the festivities, which continue all day and well into the night.

The King is Born

The next morning, we are taken to the cave's entrance and with much bowing and gesticulating we make our departure.

"Our welcome seems to have come to an end," Nicias quips.

I turn to look back at the cave entrance to the monastery and pull my horse up short. The others stop, too.

"What's wrong Basil?" Gaius.

"It's gone!"

"What's gone?"

"The cave! I can't see it!" They turn to look as well. We study the cliff. I point to where it should have been. "It's not there!"

"Was it a dream?" Nicias.

"What? We all had the same dream? It was magical, but, no, I think it was real. But where it's gone, I don't know."

Gaius grunts. "Well, are you ready to go home now Master Basilikos, or should we go look for it?" He grins. I slap him on the back.

"Let's go home!" I laugh. "I'm not ready to be a god – yet!"

Chapter Fourteen
Visiting Issaca

※❦❦❦

You already know of the artesian wellspring and the aqueducts Grandfather had built to channel water throughout the city and into little fountains in the center of each courtyard, around which different rooms are placed. At the opposite end of the courtyard from the gate is a raised dais with a latticed arbor, covered with a vine, usually grapes. The flat roofs are tiled with a low wall around its edges. We often retire to the roof in the evening as the sun sets and the heat dissipates, even sleeping there in the summer.

This is also how the Palace is built, but on a grander scale with various courtyards for the ruling family members, including harems for their women. And it sits high on the bluff's cliff, allowing many units to have windows or arched latticed openings on their dais for the vistas, and for the breezes.

Issaca's courtyard also boasted a small lake with an island and a pagoda-shaped pavilion nestled among lilies and flowering shrubs. Colorful carp swim in the waters. Doves nest in the arbor covered with medicinal vines, their gentle cooing adding to the peaceful feeling of this sanctuary.

※❦❦❦

One afternoon, not long after our experience with the Monks, I venture to my grandmother's gate. The maid who answers is shocked - men other than a husband usually don't visit the women's quarters. I request to speak to Issaca. The maid closes the gate on me. I can hear her steps running around the lake.

I'm able to hear the conversation.

"Basilikos? What on earth does your son want with me, Rachel?"

"He says he would like to visit with My Lady for a few minutes, if it is not too much of a bother." The girl's voice holds awe.

The King is Born

"Well then, show him in! A little diversion might not be a bad thing." Rachel starts to raise her shawl, but Issaca waves the motion aside and turns back to the maid. "Bring us some refreshments."

A minute later I drop to one knee and bend to kiss her outstretched hand. As I rise I drop a kiss on Mother's forehead as she pats my arm.

"Mother! I'm delighted that you are here, too!"

"Come and sit, my Grandson," Issaca points to a couch littered with cushions. "What brings you to see me in the middle of such a hot afternoon?"

"I've missed our visits, Issaca! When I was little, you and I spent so many afternoons together. Now you've retired to your rooms, and I am busy with my father and grandfather. We never see each other anymore!"

"By rights our ways have separated, Basilikos. You are a man now. You do not belong in the women's rooms."

"I know that!" I slouch against the cushion. "But I miss you, Grandmother! Our conversations were always so stimulating. Your head is filled with so much knowledge. You have seen and done and been to places I can only dream of!"

"Not so, my dear boy. You are going to do a lot of traveling in your time. You will see and understand more than any of us. You will learn great truths beyond our present comprehension." Her gaze narrows as she looks past me into the future. "You will experience great sorrow. You will make a commitment that will change your life forever. And the lives of our people." A long silence follows as the three of us ponder these words.

"You see what I mean, Issaca," I speak softly. "No one else could tell me things like this. I always thought that the divination and the sight, the discernment, all of that came down through the father's lineage. But that's not always true, is it? Grandfather has none of the powers that Father has. And now I begin to realize that I've seen them in you all along."

"You're quite right, Basil." Mother agrees. "The gifting comes from your grandmother. Before she married your grandfather, she was well known as a seer. She's still considered a prophetess, but she gave up much of her gifting when she chose to have a child."

Chapter Fourteen - Visiting Issaca

"You also will have to make choices, Basilikos," Issaca. "Some of them will be very hard to make. Others will be so easy that you will hardly even know you made them."

"But you've told me my future," I muse.

"I have only seen one possible future for you, Basilikos and in telling you as much as I have, I have overstepped my role. However, there are some things that are inevitable, and it doesn't matter what decisions you make, you will eventually travel down the same road."

The girl returns with trays of sweetmeats and cool drinks.

"Allow me to serve you, Grandmother and Mother," I say, dismissing the servant girl. Both women look surprised, then settled back against the cushions and accept my service. As I lean toward Issaca to offer her some sweetmeats, my robe falls open and Ruby swings free on her chain. Issaca reaches for the gem, turning her so that a stray beam of sunlight catches and glitters in her facets. Tiny red motes of light dance around the dais, swirl, coalesce into a stream of blood red light, which pours back into Ruby.

Issaca looks up into my eyes, a question in hers. I nod.

"You have seen it, then."

"You mean the blood, fire?" She nods. I return to my couch. "Yes. I've seen the destruction of the village and the murder of the High Priest. But Issaca . . . was that all you saw?"

"More? No! But you have?" I nod. "What have you seen?"

"A cross with a man hanging on it. I look at his face and recognize it. It is intimate to me. The love for it – for the man – is so intense, I wonder who it could possibly be. As I gaze into his eyes I see his agony. It is so deep! It knocks me to my knees. Blood flows from his side, flows down and covers me – not in a smothering way, but . . ." I hesitate for words and shrug. "I cannot explain it! But when I stand up, it's as if I'm clothed in pure white!"

"The Ultimate Sacrifice." She says after a long silence. "Rachael, have you told him of your people's belief in the Messiah?"

"Yes. From a little boy I've told him how, one day, God will send the Messiah, the Anointed One, Who will come to earth as the Son of Man, and will lay down His life for His people."

"And you think this is what I am seeing?" Both women nod.

The King is Born

"But why would I see that? Forgive me, Mother, but I don't believe in your god."

"Who is to say which god is the god you call the Most High God?" Asks Issaca. "Your mother's people believe in the Most High God whom they call El Elyon. They too, revere His name, and prefer not to use it. We have turned from the Ancient's beliefs in a plethora of gods to Zarathustra's One God. But we've also held on to many of the old beliefs, including the belief that blood must be shed to cover the sins of the people."

"I know that! I help perform the rituals each year. And you believe that one man's blood can redeem all the people?"

"Not just a man, Basil, the Son of Man, created and anointed for this specific task: to cleanse His people, once and for all!" Mother exclaims.

"You speak of the agony," Mother continues, on a different note. "Can you imagine taking on the sins of the world? How can one person bear so much for so many? I do not know!" Her face is tense with the thought. Then her expression softens. "But, oh the peace we will have in the end!"

"You feel it when you stare into the heart, don't you?" Issaca murmurs. "Sometimes I would gaze into it just to feel that peace!"

As if that peace pervades the dais, we begin to relax. But a thought suddenly brings me up straight. "I've heard that before!"

"Heard what before, Basil?" Issaca.

"Who really is the One God?" I shiver.

"I sense a story!" Issaca snuggles into the pillows. "Do tell!"

I watch her as she folds her robes gracefully across her legs. How much should I tell them? Issaca would understand, but what about mother? I decided to keep it light.

"It was in a monastery in the foothills of Gandara." Airily. "And I must warn you, Issaca, your reputation goes before you!"

"And that surprises you?" Mother laughs.

"There are many monasteries in those foothills, Basil," Issaca." And you have visited most of them!"

"This one is different! "We were being chased by a storm, lightning striking all around us. Suddenly I see a cave straight ahead

Chapter Fourteen - Visiting Issaca

of us and we dashed into it. The cave opened lead to a massive cavern that could easily hold our annual games. It was filled with monks who seemed to be waiting for someone. A small figure hopped down the stairs we'd just come down and was lifted onto a massive throne. When he uncovered his face, he looked like a ram. Even had cloven hooves for hands! And he bleated like one, too!"

"Ah! The time you healed the man gored by a bull!"

"How did you know about that!" I turn to stare at Issaca.

"We talked, remember?" She returns my gaze. I shake my head.

"I remember hearing your voice, but it was as if . . . Were you there through the night, too?"

"No," she replies. "I only answered your questions as you asked them. I knew you were fighting for his life. I presume he lived?"

"Yes, he did! It was . . . awesome!" I hesitate, wondering how to put in words what had happened that night. I glance at Mother.

"Don't worry about Rachael, Basil," Issaca chuckles. "Your mother is a lot stronger than she looks. Besides, being my daughter-in-law has taught her to accept many unusual things."

"Basil," Mother speaks gently. "Nothing you can say can shock me."

"Death was there in the room when I arrived," I watch her closely. Her face does not change. "And there was a huge Brahma bull, too.

"In that hour we call the Death Watch, Death tried to take him. I called on the One True God and Death laughed at me, demanding to know if I knew his name. All I could think of was Light. But when I was thrown to the floor, I called on . . . I called on The Most High God!" I whisper, shaken now by the memory.

"And He answered," whispers Mother. I nod.

"It was overwhelming!" I continue in a whisper. "Lightning struck and thunder shook the cave. The light caught in Ruby and filled the room, crashing and smashing into everything. It coalesced above the body, moving from head to toe and back.

"Then I realized Death had gone."

The King is Born

"That is truly splendid, Basil." Issaca, gently. We sit in silence for a very long time. Then Issaca stirs. "Now I have a story for you, Basil!" She says. "Do you know who the goat man was, and whose life you saved that day?"

"I have no idea!" I admit.

"The goat man was your grandfather eight times removed." I straighten to look at her, my mouth hanging open. How could this be? "My grandfather, six times removed," she adds.

"Yours?" I ask. She nods. "But he must be simply ancient!"

"He's reputed to be over 500 years old." She smiles and nods as I shake my head.

"No one lives to be that old! And, besides, he's so small . . . and ugly!"

"That is due to a curse," her smile deepening as she watches my expression. "The story is told that he was a tall handsome youth, much loved and admired by all of his peers. He fell in love with the most beautiful girl in the country, and she with him. Her father practiced the Black Arts and cursed him, using the one thing that he prided - his looks. He would live to be a thousand years old in the form of a ram."

"Did he marry the girl?" Issaca grins.

"We're here, aren't we?" She quips.

"Well, yes, but . . . were they married before it happened?"

She shakes her head. I shiver with distaste.

"According to legend, the beautiful young lady loved him so much that she claimed she saw no difference in him. She died in childbirth, but the son lived."

"How are we related?"

"Remember the vision of the destruction of the village that once stood here?" I nod. "The child that was abducted. His given name was Euphraino meaning 'Rejoice'. And the son is said to have died about 200 years ago after being gored by the sacrificial bull of Mithra."

"How's that possible!" I rise abruptly and walk down to the water's edge.

"It was the sacrifice of the summer solstice," she continues.

Chapter Fourteen - Visiting Issaca

"The white bull of summer. It was a huge bull, bad tempered, but flawless in every other way." Her voice fades. I know the story: The capture of the bull; the cleansing; the ceremony – all was normal until the sudden thrust of the massive head just as he slashed its throat. I see it again in slow motion.

"The blood that flowed was the bull's or the man's?

"It was both." Issaca responds to the unspoken question.

"But he died!"

"The others left him for dead." Issaca corrects me. I return to my couch.

"You mean, he didn't die. But, Issaca, that was two hundred years ago! How's this possible? How can a man survive a day after being gored by a bull, let alone two hundred years?"

"I think I missed a party!" Madjid appears at the top of the steps without a sound.

"Forgive us, my lord," Mother rises quickly, drawing her shawl over her head and across her face. I get up from the couch and stand before my grandfather.

"Madjid!" Cries his wife in delight, not moving from the pillows. "Yes, you have missed a wonderful afternoon!"

"Don't leave on my part, Rachel," he smiles at her down-turned head. "Issaca loves your visits, and I wouldn't deny either of you such pleasure." He turns to me, his tone changing. "I am surprised to find you here, Basilikos. Granted Issaca can teach you much, but do not forget that you are a man now. You have responsibilities."

"Yes, Grandfather." I bow my head, but my curiosity gets the better of me. I look up at him and ask, "How did you do that, Grandfather?"

"Do what?"

"I can see the path from here to the gate. I never saw you enter."

"Not only the Magi have their secrets, my dear Grandson!" He grins.

"We will take our leave now, my Lord," Mother turns and bows to Issaca. "Thank you, my Lady, for a wonderful afternoon."

The King is Born

"Thank you, Rachael. You are always welcome. And you, too, Basilikos. Any time you wish to discuss business," she gives me wicked smile. "Feel free to come and see me."

We leave through the gate. I feel Madjid watching us.

"Now what on earth was Basilikos doing here?" He asks.

"Remembering a childhood not so long lost," replies his wife.

"He is a good boy, I believe."

The gate closes behind us. I wave for Mother to go on without me and lean against the gate, seeing and hearing as if I am still in the dais.

"Yes, indeed he is, Madjid. Now, my dearest, what brings you in so early?"

"My love for you," he quips as he sits down beside her. "Would you be terribly upset if I said that all I really needed was some peace. It's been a terrible day, and I just need to be quiet for a while."

"Come my love," Issaca arranges herself and the pillows then raises her arms to him. "Lay your head here and allow me to ease the tension. When are you going to let go and allow Balthazar to take over? He is ready, you know."

"It's too hard to let go. A man cannot just walk away."

"As I did, you mean."

"Forgive me, I didn't mean to hurt you."

"You didn't. You are right, though. I am sure it is much harder for a man to abdicate. What would you do with yourself? You couldn't very well take up weaving or embroidery, now, could you?" She smiles down into the tired old face cradled in her lap.

"No." He chuckles. "All I'd manage to do is make a nuisance of myself everywhere. No! No! I shall continue to run this city until I drop dead! I pray the Mighty One that will be a long time from now."

He closes his eyes and is quickly asleep. Issaca lies holding him, stroking his hair and beard. Tears well in her eyes.

※

Chapter Fifteen
Helping Madjid

～♡♡～

What I watched in Issaca's courtyard continues to disturb me greatly, especially since I am now eighteen and my place is beside my Father in the Council. I watch Grandfather Madjid, beginning to understand how the toll of this place, hot and noisy, seething with bitterness and unrest, is affecting him. After the first week, I am ready to retreat to the quiet and simple ways of the Temple, better yet, to run for the hills!

"Basil," Father catches up with me as I hurry away from the Hall. "Wait for me! Let me walk with you."

"I need fresh air, Father!" I say over my shoulder.

"So do I!" He joins me as I head for the dais in his courtyard.

"How can you stand this day after day?" I ask in frustration.

"It's not always like this!" Father drops on a divan. A servant brings cool drinks and fruit. Father waits for him to leave. "In the beginning, there was just Madjid and his brothers, Kasim, Hiram and -"

"It wouldn't have been so bad if we hadn't all been so prolific!" Madjid growls as he comes striding up the steps.

"Madjid!" Neither of us had heard his approach.

"Don't bother!" He waves us down. "It's too hot and tempers are too short for civilities!"

He flings himself onto a divan and claps his hands for service.

"Bring me a drink and some sweet meats. None of this fruit!" He snaps, waving it away.

"Between us we had twenty-four sons." He continues. "The the plague took two brothers and many of their brood. I should have turned the lot of them out, let them go back to the Steppes and the nomadic life, but, there is safety in numbers." He pauses to drink.

The King is Born

"They all have become good fighting men.

"Now I have those fellows, plus Balthazar's seven brothers! And they are all greedy, blood-sucking lizards!" He gulps down his drink and calls for another.

"So, what are we going to do about this mess, humm?" He demands, glowering at both of us. "Magus Balthazar and young Basilikos of the Temple! What have you got to say?"

I glance at Father. He sits twirling his cup.

"Go ahead, Basil!" Without looking up. "You have something to say."

"Grandfather," I hesitate.

"Yes! Yes, boy, speak up! Don't simper like a silly female. If you have something to say, say it!"

"How were things done when your family roamed the Steppes?"

"What's that got to do with anything?!" He demands, testily.

"You are trying to handle all the problems of the whole city. I don't believe that is the way our ancestor Shahazad would have done it."

"Life on the Steppes was totally different to life in a walled city!" Madjid's voice was still irritable. "My Grandfather, Shahazad left his father's tribe and started his own with eight sons. My father, Jenghiz was the eldest son, and in time broke away to form his own tribe. I was his eldest. Kasim, Hiram and I had different mothers, but we are very close in age and inseparable! We were out hunting with our other brothers when it happened. The camp was destroyed in one night of terror - like the village that once stood here. Only a few survived the attack: The High Priest and those who had found sanctuary with him in a cave. Issaca had Balthazar with her on one of her trips into the hills to gather herbs." He pauses for a moment, lost in the memories.

"We found those that were left and came south, looking for a safer place to live. I had often heard rumors of ruins in the mists above Bactra, and I had a desire to put down roots, stay in one place for more than one summer."

"Did the ways of your Grandfather work?" I ask.

Chapter Fifteen - Helping Madjid

"What?" He glares at me, annoyed at the interruption.

"How did Shahazad run the camp?"

"Each man was accountable for his own family. Issues between brothers were taken to Shahazad. Well, yes, I suppose his ways did well enough. But times are different now. We are not nomads."

"The concept is the same. You are the High Council, as was Shahazad. Create a General Council made up of your brothers who preside over their own sons, who preside over their own sons, on down the line to individual families. Each level decides the less serious issues. As with Shahazad, issues are taken up the chain of command. The High Council is the last resort before the issue come to you. Your word is final."

The silence is complete.

Madjid chuckles. "My word is final. You hear that, Balthazar?" He looks at me. "You are wise for your age, Basilikos. This is good!"

⁓❂⁓

Madjid is quick to act on my suggestion and called a meeting of all his brothers and their sons and their sons for the next morning in his chambers. Each brother's sons and grandsons sit in a family group.

As Madjid lays out his plan before his brothers, I watch the men with interest. Kasim nods as Grandfather speaks, his lips pursed in thought. Hiram is a little agitated. Timaeus and the other three could obviously care less, their disrespect for their brother thinly veiled by their expressions. And it showed in their offspring as well.

"It worked for our forefathers, it should work for us," Kasim is positive.

"Yes, but," Hiram prowls the room, hesitant. "Things are different now. There are so many of us. How will we keep control?"

"You think we have control now?" Demands Madjid.

"How can we be sure that all are treated equally?" Hiram continues. "I remember the way it was – not good! Tyranny ruled in each family. There was abuse." He begins to wring his hands.

The King is Born

"Uncle Hiram," Father speaks gently. "There is no way of knowing what will happen behind the walls of each dwelling. We don't control that now. Nor will we in the future. We must trust in the integrity of each man." Timaeus snorts. Thales, his son imitates him. Hiram shakes his head and walks out the door.

"Why is Hiram so upset by this?" I ask. "What was the abuse he refers to?"

"There is always abuse of some kind or other!" Timaeus, impatiently. "The stronger prey on the weaker. Hiram is weak!"

"Hiram is not weak!" Father retorts. "Hiram is gentle, thoughtful, and kind."

"I have never seen him take part in the games," I muse. "I cannot think that I have ever seen him out in the fields. What does he do with his time?"

"Hiram," Grandfather breaks off as Hiram returns.

"I don't know if I could rule my descendants," Hiram says flatly.

"You would not have to, Uncle Hiram," Balthazar assures him. "The General Council would support you."

"All right," Hiram nods. "I guess it might work."

"Good, now let's get down to business." Madjid calls for the scribes, and we settle to the matter at hand.

Our ideas have worked well – too well. The High Council now only convenes two days a week. Madjid has all the peace in the world and all the time he could possibly want in which to do nothing. But of course, he can not do nothing. He begins to meddle, talking at first to one brother and then to another. He seems to thrive on mischief, and delights in taunting his sons and nephews, one against another. Of course, that means more issues came to the High Council which gives him more to do, so he is kept happy.

Chapter Sixteen
The Arrival of the Wise Men

❦

Madjid sits alone in one of two Roman Curules - a chair with heavy, curved, crossed legs supporting low armrests. The one next to him is vacant. Basil stands close by. The chamber is filling with men in ones, twos and small groups. Basil steps close to Madjid and whispers.

"I will go and look for my father, Grandfather."

Madjid nods and Basil slips away, heading for his father's chambers. When he arrives, he finds Balthazar sitting at his big table muttering to himself as he squints at sheets of scribbled notes. Star charts and maps are spread across the rest of the clutter. He looks exhausted, his clothing disheveled as if he hasn't bathed or changed clothes in several days.

"What's happening to you, Father!" I forget respect. "Grandfather is waiting for you in the Council Chamber. The Emissary from Persia will be presented at any moment!"

"Eh, what?" Still studying his notes.

"Father!"

"Oh, yes, right." He puts his quill down. "I'd completely forgotten." He looks at the mess on the table and sighs. "I suppose I should go down and join Madjid, right?"

"Father! What's so important that you've completely lost track of everything?" My tone should have angered Father, but it doesn't seem to faze him in the least.

"I've been studying this star. About nine months ago I first saw it, hanging there in the south-western sky. Every night, there it was, not moving as others do. That is unusual enough, but then I noticed something else. I used that tube with glass in it the Egyptian trader sold me. It magnifies the sky so that I can see the stars better."

The King is Born

"So, I ask you again! What's so important about this particular star that you forget everything around you, embarrass your own family and risk a breach with Persia?"

"This star is so big and bright that I believe it is a Natal Star." He waves at the tables."All these manuscripts. I've sent messages to many Magi. Finally, messages from two arrived. Come and see for yourself. – Come!" As a knock on the door interrupts.

Josias, Father's servant enters.

"Sir, two caravans have just arrived. Two noblemen are at the gates asking for you, Sir. They say they are Magi from far countries."

"Excellent! They've made good time! Take them to the guest quarters and get them food and drink. Then when they're ready, show them in here. I'll go get cleaned up. Basil –"

"My Lord, forgive me, but the guest quarters are full! The Emissary from Persia and his people . . .!"

"Oh! Oh, yes!" He turns to me, confusion marring his face. I take charge.

"Josias, find my servant and tell him to get my rooms ready for two honored guests. It's not what Magi would expect, but there are two sleeping rooms and the day room. Then go to the Magi and make Father's apologies and take them to my rooms."

Josias is half way out the door.

"No – wait!" I turn to Father. "Father, with your leave, I'll go and speak to these men, myself. I will explain what is happening and ask for their consideration." Turning back to Josias. "Josias, after you have found my servant, go to my Grandfather and explain to him what has happened. Don't say anything about Father not being ready. Let him think he's taking care of these men. And when you have done that, go to the kitchens and have them prepare a meal for these men."

Josias glances from Father to me, bows and leaves on the run.

"Come Father, let's get you cleaned up. And you can tell me who am I entertaining." I hustle Father into his bathing room, helping him off with his robes.

"These are the two Magi I was telling you about. They are both very learned and speak Greek, so you'll have no problem

Chapter Sixteen - The Arrival of the Wise Men

talking to them." As he steps under the running water, he calls back to me. "Can you get some clean things out for me, please?"

"I'm off now," I say as I drop the clean clothes on a bench.

"Basil! Thank you! You are a good son."

I pause at the door. "I don't understand, but it's important to you. Father, we desperately need your expertise with this Emissary!"

"Don't worry, my son, I'll be all right now."

I close the door behind me and hurry down to the Caravansary.

The Caravansary is built outside the city gates. It's a large, flat, cobbled courtyard with water and feeding troughs and tethering posts. On the two long sides are camel and horse stalls as well as tack rooms. The far end houses bunk rooms for the camel drivers. The fourth side has a low wall along it with a double gate in the middle.

As I approach the chaos of three caravans trying to sort things out. I easily pick out the two Magi as they are leaning against the low wall, observing.

I approach and bow to them.

"My Lords! I am Basilikos, son of Magus Balthazar. Please forgive the lack of a proper welcome! Madjid and Father are in conference with a Persian Emissary who arrived yesterday morning."

"Basilikos son of Balthazar. We were not expected. We cannot be offended!"

"If it would be easier for all, we can camp in the fields outside the gates."

"Oh, no, my Lords!" Horrified. "That would not do at all! There is plenty of room for you. The quarters to which I will take you are a little less than you would normally occupy, but..."

"This is generous, Basilikos. Another night out on the mountain is not all that appealing."

"Forgive us, Master Basilikos, we have not introduced ourselves. I am Cheng Sherong from a far province of China, and this is Gandophares of India."

I acknowledge the introductions and lead them through the main gates towards the palace.

The King is Born

"This city has a history, I believe. I hope we may see more of it before we leave." The one called Gandophares says.

"People have inhabited this site for hundreds of years because of the fine artesian well. It is large enough to provide water throughout the city."

"And how is that done?" Gandophares' interest intensifies.

I point to an aqueduct but keep moving.

"Father had Roman aqueducts such as this one built throughout the city."

"I have heard stories of these - troughs!" Cheng Sherong is intrigued.

"Aqueducts have allowed our tribe to expand and live comfortably. But there is only so much water. Our population has grown too rapidly. As my generation begins to produce families, we are going to have to find more water - or move."

"A problem for desert dwellers. But not a problem we have in my country." Cheng Sherong chuckles.

"Or mine! When the monsoons come, we have too much water!"

"This I must hear more about," politely, but too much water is the last thing I want to hear about. I suppress a shudder.

"The rain begins to fall and does not stop for days at a time. The streets flow with water. Sickness and disease run rampant." Gandophares continues.

"Too much of a good thing!" I murmur, pushing open the gate to my own courtyard and leading the two men inside.

"My Lords, this humble courtyard and all its rooms are at your disposal. There are two sleeping rooms, a bathing room, a study and, of course, the dais at the far end. I hope that they will meet your needs."

Josias steps through the gate behind us.

"Josias, my father's servant will be here shortly with refreshments. He is at your disposal. Josias has traveled the known world with my father and is familiar with the customs of other peoples."

Chapter Sixteen - The Arrival of the Wise Men

"You do your father great honor, Basilikos!" Cheng Sherong bows to me.

"Truly, my lords, it is my pleasure to serve you. When you have rested and eaten, send Josias for me. If my father is still occupied with the Emissary, I would be delighted to show you the Palace and the city, or anything else that would amuse you. Until then, my Lords, I bid you farewell."

༺❤༻

When I return some hours later, the two are lounging on the dais. Josias is cleaning up the remains of a meal.

"My Lords, I do hope that all your needs have been provided, and that you have rested and are refreshed."

"Thank you, Basilikos. Yes, your servant has been the essence of hospitality!" Gandophares assures me.

"Father is free to see you if you would care to come with me?"

We head back out into the palace, heading towards Father's rooms.

When we enter, we find Father standing in front of the cluttered table. I introduce the Magi and step back, leaning against a bit of wall not covered with shelving.

"You honor me greatly by coming so quickly, my Lords. Please forgive me for not greeting you immediately upon your arrival. I hope that everything was acceptable to you, and that you are rested."

"Yes, my Lord Magus Balthazar, we could not have asked for more." Cheng Sherong.

Gandophares turns to me as he speaks.

"We owe you a debt of gratitude, Basilikos, for I understand we occupy your rooms." I bow slightly in acknowledgment as Father leads them to chairs set in around the big table. He takes his seat, and I step up just behind and to the right of him.

"I have allowed Basilikos to attend our meeting as he is learning about the stars."

"It's good to see the young taking such an interest!" Turning to me. "Your Father has told you that this is possibly a Natal Star announcing the birth of someone very significant to our world?"

The King is Born

"He's told me that it is a Heraldic Sign, yes, but more than that, I do not know, yet."

Father is searching through some scrolls. Finding the one he wants, he unrolls it.

"Since I last wrote to you, I've purchased a scroll from an Israelite. It includes the writings of some of their prophets. My wife is an Israelite and has helped me translate them."

"Your wife!" Gandophares, startled. "She is knowledgeable in these matters?"

"Yes. Rachel is very intelligent and even now is still full of curiosity." Both men mutter and shake their heads. Father ignores it and continues speaking. "The Israelites declare that a Messiah - Christ in the Greek meaning the Anointed One of God will be born and his birth heralded by a Natal Star. They say He will be the Savior of the World."

"The whole world?" Startled, I interrupt. "Or just the Israelites?"

"But that is debatable. For, according to our traditions, he is only a great teacher, prophet, and healer, nothing more." Gandophares.

"You've heard of this man before?" Father.

"Our prophets speak of such a man. A Zealot, a fanatic, who makes wild claims. It is true that he will be a powerful man, a prophet, teacher, and healer. But the Savior of the whole world? Humph!" Cheng Sherong.

Gandophares leans forward. "Balthazar, why do you bring this person to our attention now?"

"The star hasn't grown any larger for about a week."

"If it's stopped growing and is holding steady," Gandophares interrupts. "That must mean the child is born! Let's not waste any more time."

The three men rise and head for the door, Father speaking as they go.

"We can start tonight if you so wish. My servants began readying my caravan this morning when you arrived."

"Good! Then there's no need to tarry!" Gandophares, eagerly.

Chapter Sixteen - The Arrival of the Wise Men

I step forward to block the door, alarmed.

"Father! Please! You've forgotten the Emissary from Persia! You are to dine with him tonight. "Please! This man must not be offended. Surely one more day won't make that much difference!"

Father pauses to study me, then turns to the others.

"I'm afraid Basil is right. I must consider my people's needs. Would you mind waiting one more day?" Both men nod in agreement.

"By all means, dine with him, Balthazar! The Emissary may know something about this child king!"

"Excellent idea! You must attend! It's not long before the banquet. If you will permit Basilikos to take you to your quarters..."

༺♥༻

As the dinner hour neared, I collect the Magi and lead them through the palace to the Central Court. As we enter the great colonnade, we see Father and Mother coming toward us. They are holding hands and whispering to each other. Mother sees us first and quickly covers her face as Father greets the Magi.

"It is a sad custom you have, Magus Balthazar, to hide your beautiful women from view," Cheng Sherong as he bows to Mother.

"Yes, indeed it is," adds Gandophares. "In my country, we parade them for everyone to see. It is a great honor to have many beautiful wives."

"In our country, we protect our women from leering eyes and unwanted advances," I speak hotly.

"Perhaps we do carry our customs to extremes," Father gives my shoulder a sharp squeeze. "We keep them behind walls and insist they cover themselves in public. One day, we may all find a way to live happily with our women, and respect them as we do ourselves." Mother bows to the men and slips away to the women's quarters. She will be entertaining the Persian women tonight.

"You talk as if women are our equals, Balthazar!" Exclaims Cheng Sherong.

"Why not?" Father challenges. "Some of them have keen minds. And, although their logic is very different from ours, it is amazing to listen to them. Of course, I have been spoiled with my

The King is Born

mother and my wife. I am well aware that not all women are so intelligent."

"Women are no more than chattel!" Cheng Sherong, dismissively. "They have been put on this earth for our enjoyment, to fill our senses and our every need. Who needs an intelligent woman?"

Father's hand is still on my shoulder. His fingers tighten in warning before I can respond.

"It is obvious we differ in opinions about women, but it is safe to say that without them life would be very dull indeed!" Father says with a smile.

"I must agree with that!" Laughs Gandophares. "Come, Cheng Sherong! We have much more important things to discuss than women."

"And here is the Emissary from Persia. Allow me to introduce you." Father moves smoothly away from dangerous ground. He glances at me. My face feels as if it is carved out of granite, but I know he can see the anger in my eyes. He winks, then turns to introduce the Emissary and the Magi.

The Emissary from Persia knew nothing of the prophecies of a child king born to be the Savior of the World. He rather seemed to think it was amusing and began to make fun of the Magi for wasting their time. Once again Father eased the tension by turning the conversation to other matters. But for the three Magi the evening was a total waste of time. I could tell that Father longed to be off, a sense of urgency stirring in his blood.

The talks with the Emissary the next morning found Father in no better frame of mind. He managed to negotiate and sign a treaty in record time. By noon, the meetings were finished. Father left Madjid to say the farewells and headed back to his rooms.

Chapter Seventeen
The Departure of the Wise Men

ଔଓଓଽ

Cheng Sherong and Gandophares, rising later, have enjoyed a leisurely morning. When they are finally ready, they call for me and I take them to Father's study, where they pore over the maps on the table. Neither man had been this far west before, and they will have to depend upon Father for the best route.

"Good morning, my Lords!" Father bursts through the door. The relief from finishing business and getting back to the Star is tangible. "I hope you slept well and have had a comfortable morning."

"Yes, thank you, my Lord Balthazar," Gandophares. "We were very comfortable last night. Your accommodations are very gracious, indeed."

"Yes," agrees Cheng Sherong. "Forgive us for intruding on your study, my Lord."

"Not at all!" Father drops the formal voice as the excitement takes hold. "I see you are looking at the maps. I've charted a route that I believe will be the quickest. Our joined caravans will be large enough to discourage the average robber. However, the size will also slow us down considerably."

"If speed is important, we could leave some of our people here, if that would be all right with you," Gandophares.

"What do you think? If the Star has stopped growing and the child is born already, we obviously cannot be there for his birth. Is it so important that we hurry?" Father muses.

"I don't believe so," Cheng Sherong. "I think safety is an important factor here. Also, we are Magi. We cannot be running around the desert, as do the Bedouins. When we present ourselves to this King, we should do so with pomp and pageantry, otherwise we won't be received with due respect."

The King is Born

"Very true," Father studies the maps. "Then I believe this is the way we should go. We will follow the trade route as far as the Caspian Sea, through the Aria and Parthia Mountain Ranges. These are arid mountains, so, even at this time of the year we shouldn't have a problem with snow. And the route follows several different rivers, so there will be plenty of water. We will follow the trade route around the Southern end of the Caspian Sea until we reach this river here," he points to a river that runs into the Caspian Sea from the south. "At this point, we can take the long way around, following the trade route until we reach Armenia. From there, we could take any one of the well-traveled routes south to Jerusalem. Or -" he traces a line due south from the Caspian Sea. "We can go straight south from here, following this river up into the mountains. There's a pass here that will take us through to the other side, where we can follow the Diyala River to the Tigris. There we can join the Persian Royal Road heading west until we cross the Euphrates River. From there, we turn south and follow the trade route through Damascus and on to Jerusalem." We all study the routes in silence.

"How long do you think it will take us?" Cheng Sherong.

"If we go through Armenia, it will take us a good two years. The route is long and circumnavigates many mountain ranges. However, if we go due south, we can cut off several months, easily."

"Why not go south instead of turning west onto the Royal Road? That seems to be taking us out of our way," Gandophares taps the map.

"Yes, it will. But we will stay within the Median Empire. If we continued south - and that route is a good one - we would enter Babylonia. And since Babylonia and Media are at war, this would be a very risky route to take. However, it is the fastest way."

"Speed is important, but not at the risk of our lives or the lives of our men," Cheng Sherong, firmly. "We will take the middle route."

"Good. Then that's settled." Father rolls up the maps. "My Lords, I don't believe there is anything else to say or do." The others agree. "Then let's get started!"

༺♥༻

"My Lords!" I greet the Magi as they entered the Main Square. "The caravans are just about ready."

Chapter Seventeen - The Departure of the Wise Men

"Good!" Father claps me on the back. "We'll be leaving right away."

"I thought we were going to wait until this evening when the Star would be out to follow." I speak up.

"No need for that. We know the general direction for now, and since the desert to the South is still fiercely hot, we will go West to the Caspian Sea then turn south."

"So, you are determined to chase this Star!" Madjid joins us. With him are Issaca and Mother.

"Father!" Balthazar exclaims. "You have come to see us off! Thank you, my Lord. Do we have your blessings?"

"You have my blessings, my son," sighs the old man. "I think it foolish. But Issaca said you must go; it is part of your destiny. So, go! But you will be sorely missed."

"Not too much, I think," Father grins. "You have Issaca and Basilikos to help you. You won't miss me for long."

"Father!" I cry. "You said I could go on your next journey. You can't go back on your promise!"

"You're not going!" Exclaims Mother. "It's bad enough that your father's going on such a foolish journey. You are certainly not going to go. That is final!"

"Father!" This as Mother grabs my arm and pulls me back.

"Rachael!" The authority in Father's voices stops all protest. Mother drops my arm and bows her head. Issaca steps to her side and puts her arm around her.

"Basilikos! Walk with me a moment." Father leads me away from the others. "Basilikos, I know I told you that you could go on the next journey, but I really think that this one is a little bit much for your first trip. I know, I know!" He stems the rush of angry words. "We don't know exactly what we're getting into. We do know that the Medes and Babylonians are at war. And we do know that the Israelites are a fierce people. Although they've been conquered by the Romans, that doesn't mean they are subdued. They've been known to take matters into their own hands more often than not." He turns and places both hands on my shoulders, looking me in the eye.

The King is Born

"Have you forgotten so quickly, my victories last summer?!" The outrage has me trembling. "How I won every single event in the games with cunning and wisdom? You need me!"

"Tournaments are not battle. Between the three of us we have a full army attending us. Besides," he glances back at the others. I interrupt.

"Who's going to take care of the injured? Huh? Can even you beat my miraculous life-saving success like the man gored by a bull?"

"No," exasperation. "I have not forgotten your accomplishments of the last few years. You've proven yourself time and again. And this week you showed diplomacy in handling the unexpected arrival of the Magi while I was lost in my study of the Star."

"Another point for me!"

"You are needed here!"

"Ha!"

"Madjid needs you here by his side. He's a tired old man. I am going to be gone for two to four years. If something should happen to him while I am gone, your uncles would try and take over. That would be a disaster for our whole tribe!"

"And your mother needs you. Now, don't give me that look! You know she counts on you still."

"She has Issaca! She doesn't need me!" I try to pull away, but Father grips my shoulders with an authority I have seldom experienced.

"Listen!" He demands. "Your mother is not as strong as you think. She tries to hide it from us, but she forgets who we are. She cannot do it all."

"She's stronger than you think! Besides, she's a woman and she has Issaca."

"OK. Look! I need you to stay for my own peace of mind. I may be gone for several years. Madjid could die of old age before I return. With all you have learned and all you have accomplished; I know our city will be safe in your care. Please! Do it for me?"

Chapter Seventeen - The Departure of the Wise Men

I slump in defeat, kicking at a stone with a sigh, and nod, glumly. Father eases his grip on my arms and pats my back, then returns to the others.

I turn and head for the city gates.

Chapter Eighteen
The Annual Games

❦

I'm sitting on the top of a ridge overlooking the plateau that supports the city of Madjid

Just as then, now I could see past the rooftops of Madjid, to the distant green hills of the city of Bactres, a truly magnificent gem. In the clear, clean light of early spring, I make out the rooftops and see the graceful curve of palms. Boats dot the river. A caravan is making its way out of the South Gate toward the Roman Road where it might continue to the south, or may turn and head west.

In the foreground, by contrast, the fortified city of Madjid looks stark and uninviting. Perched on the edge of the cliff overlooking the Oxus River, the massive walls of native clay and stone hide all but the feathery tips of palms from the casual observer.

I take a deep breath, scenting orange blossoms, verbena, hemp, and smile as I remember that time upon this ridge. Father and I had been riding together out across the foothills and into the Hindu Kush. We had stopped in this very same spot.

"Smell that, Basilikos," Father had said, himself taking a deep breath. "What do you smell?"

"Hot sand," I had replied promptly.

"What else?" When I did not answer, he continued. "Verbena, hemp, orange blossoms. I tell you, Basilikos, there's no better land than this! Look how the setting sun catches the ridges of the mountains. Look how the waters foam white as the two rivers meet. See the glimmer of the sun on the Oxus River as it flows north across the desert? I tell you, it's magnificent!"

"Look, Father, I can just make out the minarets of Bactres! I love going there! It's such a fine city. I bet it's every bit as fine as Rome!"

The King is Born

"Now that's a city! One day I'll take you there."

He had urged his camel forward and I had followed. As we wound our way down the steep hillside into the deepening dusk, I pulled up level with him.

"Tell me how Grandfather built this place, please, Father."

"Our people weren't always a settled tribe, you know. When I was young, we wandered over the mighty Steppes. We migrated with the changing seasons.

"But one day, Father found this place. Oh, it wasn't anything like it is now. See the orchards nestled under the mighty wall? They weren't there. In fact, the wall wasn't even there. When we first saw it, all that was here was a muddy pool left from the clogged artesian well and a crumbling marble wall that overlooked the confluence of the two tributaries."

"But Grandfather had a hunch, didn't he?"

"Yes, he did. He had the men clean out that muddy old pond. They pulled out all sorts of stuff from the old village, including a few bones."

"Human bones?"

"Well, could have been!" He had grinned at me as I pulled my camel closer to his, the darkness closing in around us. "But after more than five hundred years, bones is bones!" He had laughed a fiendish laugh, his teeth flashing in the gloom.

"Back then," he had continued after a moment. "Bands of Medes, Persians and Turks roamed the Steppes. No one was safe. That is why we built the massive wall as high as two houses and a full room thick. And the only known way to enter is still through that massive gates of wood fortified with iron bars, you can't burn them down and you can't break them down!"

A wolf howled from the hillside above us, The camels increased their pace.

"And we can't get behind them any too soon!" I had said, pushing my camel even closer to his. That had made him laugh, too, more of an indulgent chuckle.

A full moon hung low in the eastern sky, smiling benevolently at the scene before it, sweeping a silver paintbrush across the

Chapter Eighteen - The Annual Games

grasslands and making the stones on the windswept slopes of the Hindu Kush stand out in relief.

The massive walls of Madjid loomed above us as those mighty gates swung open and our camels moved swiftly toward a warm bed and a full manger.

"I happen to know, Father," I had spoken softly, not wanting to dispel the illusion. "That it was you who suggested emptying the pool. It was you who found the bones of that first high priest with the Ruby Heart still around his neck. It was you and Grandmother who saw the vision of his death. You try to pass it off lightly, but I know what part you played in the building of this city!"

"Ah, but it doesn't tell as well!" He responded on a chuckle.

༺♡༻

My thoughts return to the happenings of today. Below me those massive gates are wide open with people coming and going. Outside the gates, the caravansary is full of horses and camels, the overflow tethered to the low retaining wall.

On the field closer to me are two rows of tents that have been arranged, their sides thrown back to allow the soft spring breezes to blow through. Thick Persian rugs and large pillows cushion the hard ground where men recline in groups watching the games and enjoying a veritable feast.

In the tents nearer the gates, the women and girls are grouped. The sides of these tents are of a soft, gauzy material that allows them privacy, but permits them to watch, too. Close to them the younger children play, their ayahs keeping a watchful eye over them.

What holds the crowd's attention on this day and for several days' past, are the games of a tribe in peaceful times, meant to keep the fighting men's skills honed razor-sharp, and to introduce the younger men to the thrill of battle. Every weapon has been tested - the bow and arrow, the javelin, the swords, long and short, the ax, the pike. Every test of speed, skill and strength has been undertaken with gusto - wrestling, hand-to-hand combat, foot races, camel and horse races, anything and everything in which two or more men can compete! Only one test remains: the final horse-mounted dual.

The King is Born

One rider pitted against another in mortal combat. In true battle, the object of such a duel would be to kill the opponent as quickly as possible, before he could kill you, but in peaceful times like these, when skill, competency, horsemanship, speed and agility are put to the supreme test, a ribbon tied to the breastplate of the contender is the ultimate prize.

I have excelled through all the games, as I had done last year, before Father had left on his quest for the Baby King. I am one of two finalists of the mounted games. I have made it through all the trials. Now, I am to meet the best man in my grandfather's army. Cyrus, one of my uncles, is a big man on a big horse. He's known for his fierceness in battle and his ruthless reputation goes before him, making many a brave man step aside as he passes by.

It is time. I pat Altyn's neck. He's a Golden Horse, called so because of the bright sheen to his coat. He's intelligent, agile, and fast, and has the staying power needed in the hunt or in battle. I've trained him well for hands-free battle, so as I squeeze his sides, he moves into a trot, seeming to float over the ground, his angular body morphing into a sinuous line. Pressure on his right side, and he turns to the right. Two quick squeezes, and he spins, returning the way we'd just come. Digging my toes into his sides brings him up short, two taps and he turns again.

"Hi-i!" I hiss at him, and he bursts into a full gallop, his body dropping closer to the ground as his long legs stretch out, eating up the distance.

"Master Basilikos!" My servant, Hammed comes running to my side as I dismount at the end of the field. "The Final Event! Where have you been!?"

"I went for a ride."

"But, Master, your horse will be tired and will do poorly! I'll see if I can find you another."

"That won't be necessary, Hammed. You should know by now that I won't ride any other horse into battle! Come along! Help me get dressed." I pass the reigns to a livery hand and head for my tent.

Chapter Eighteen - The Annual Games

We sit on our mounts at opposite ends of the field, waiting for the command to fight. I feel strangely detached, as if I am only an observer. I put my hand over Ruby, drawing comfort for the touch. The confidence not only comes from being well prepared to meet this man, Cyrus, a tough trainer, not accepting weakness or ineptness as an excuse. In more recent years, I have watched him as he drills his troops, as he works his horse, as he pushes himself. He is fierce and a frightening sight when the rage is upon him, and the smell of blood is in his nostrils.

Our armor is the same: a bronze helmet with a leather lining and scale-like attachments to protect the nose bridge and the temples, and a lethal spike on the top; a breastplate and shin guards made of woven leather and bronze, and, strapped to the left arm a bronze shield covered with woven leather strips. It, too, has a bronze spike at its center, making it a weapon as well as protection. The actual weapon of choice is a scimitar, a two-edged razor-sharp curved blade that ends with a pointed tip.

"On your marks!" Booms the man with the signal flag. Hammed guides my horse to its mark, glancing back at me as I draw my scimitar. The blade glistens in the sun. The jewels in the handle sparkle. I sit tall and straight in my saddle, my chin tucked into the armor, my eyes brilliant with a sudden thrill of excitement. I nod to Hammed. He lets go of the reigns and steps aside.

The flag flutters to the ground. I signal Altyn, and he leaps forward, charging toward our opponent. The distance stretches endlessly before me, Altyn seeming to move in slow motion as the advancing rider rushes toward me, his voice raised in a battle cry that curdles the air. I move toward him in silence, waiting, watching, knowing his every move.

It happens quickly. He's upon me, swinging his scimitar. I raise my shield, his blade penetrating it, jarring my whole body. As he moves away, he wrenches his sword out of my shield, almost unseating me.

I give Altyn's two quick squeezes. He spins, presenting his protected side to Cyrus whose slower mount is just beginning its turn. I raise my scimitar and start the swing. His reflexive moves brings his shield up, crashing against mine, almost unseating me again. I dig my knees into Altyn's sides to keep seated. He takes it as

The King is Born

a signal and sweeps round on his haunches so quickly that we almost rear-end Cyrus' horse. I thrust my scimitar under Cyrus' shield and neatly hook the flying ribbon.

Cyrus continues his turn and starts back. Altyn prances with the adrenaline. I raise my scimitar with his ribbon on its tip and shout, "Your ribbon, my Lord!"

A gasp, then a cheer explode from the watching crowd as Cyrus looks down at his empty breastplate. I turn Altyn again. He floats toward the entrance of the center tent, his feet rising high in the victory prance. In front of the tent, he stops. I lean slightly forward, and Altyn arches his neck as he extends his right foreleg, drawing up his left until his nose touches his knee. The crowd explodes with more cheers as I dismount and face Grandfather Madjid as he comes forward to present the Champion's Wreath.

"Well done! Well done, indeed! You have excelled this day, young Basilikos. It gives me great honor to place the Champion's Wreath upon your head. I pray the Mighty One that you will show such courage in the day of battle!"

"Thank you, my Lord!" I bow my head to receive the wreath, hardly containing the adrenaline as the triumph still courses through my veins. I leap back onto Altyn's back, turning him to face the row of all the other combatants that had formed behind me. A few paces in front of the line, my opponent, still seated on his steed, watches me.

Altyn high-steps to Cyrus' mount and, without prompting, bows. As I bow low over his neck, I catch the glitter in Cyrus' eyes. He salutes me.

"I sense intense anger and hatred," Ruby confirms my own feelings.

"Cyrus doesn't like to lose!" I respond as I canter Altyn to one end of the row of combatants where Gaius and Nicias wait eagerly to greet me. Altyn prances sideways as we move along the row. At the end of the row I brandish my scimitar, a warrior's cry bursting from my throat and echoed from the line of men. I race around the arena, Cyrus and all the contestants following.

Chapter Eighteen - The Annual Games

"You did well, Basilikos," Cyrus comments as we lead our horses out of the ring. "The gods are surely with you."

"No, my lord. I mean, yes, of course they were. But, I know your weakness."

"Careful!" Cries Ruby.

"My weakness!" Cyrus' face reddens.

"Agh! Ruby! I'm wild!" I duck my head.

"Forgive my Grandson, my lord Cyrus!" Madjid joins us just in time! "It is the excitement. He does not mean to insult you."

"Madjid!" The two men greet each other. "Of course, he doesn't, my Lord. As you say, it's the excitement. He! He! He!" The laugh is not convincing.

"We were young and brash once, weren't we?" Grandfather continues to make peace as Cyrus offers me his hand. I take it, looking into his eyes. I hear his thoughts, so intense, I see them being enacted:

The city of Madjid shrouded in a gray cloud, the fields barren, the orchards dead. Cyrus, as the Army Commander, rides through the city gates ahead of an army, barring the way for the returning Magi to enter.

Hoping I haven't shown the shock running through me, I release his hand and turn to give Altyn's reigns to Hammed.

"Do you really know his secret, my lord?" Hammed asks in awe.

"Hmm? What?" Still reeling from shock. Behind his back, Hammed makes the sign to ward off evil. I have to smile. "Relax, Hammed! Cyrus is a hard master, to his men, to himself, and especially to his horse. Always be kind to your horse," I add absently and needlessly, because Hammed will never own a horse." I stop short, frowning and shaking my head.

"What's wrong? You're as pale as - you've seen something, haven't you?" Hammed's face pales as well.

"I must go to Issaca immediately!" I break into a run toward the city gates.

Chapter Nineteen
The Journey Begins

❦

When I reach Issaca's workroom, I knock and enter without waiting for permission. Issaca is hanging herbs to dry. She pauses to welcome me, but instead demands, "What is it?"

I'm not sure, but I saw something just now."

"Here, sit down." She dips a cup in a bucket of water and offers it to me. I gulp it down, pass the cup back to her and begin to pace the room.

"Father mentioned hearing rumors of a plot to take over Madjid." I rub my hands over my face and mouth. "I think I just found out proof!"

"How? What?"

"I shook hands with Cyrus and had a vision of Madjid in ruins and the fields decimated. And that's not all! Ruby says something's amiss with Father and the Baby King."

Issaca glances down at Ruby hanging against my chest.

"Ruby, what can you tell us?"

Ruby appears in a ray of light from the gemstone. Issaca raises her eyebrows in surprise.

"This is new!" But Ruby doesn't bother to explain.

"I didn't see so much as get impressions. Women weeping, the streets littered with little dead bodies. I get the strong impression that Balthazar and the Baby he seeks are in mortal danger."

"Was this from Creator?" Issaca.

"He did not tell me in words. I only saw-"

"Impressions! Both of you!" Issaca shakes her head.

"What Basil saw – it may just be wishful thinking on Cyrus' part – "

The King is Born

"Not important!" Issaca waves it aside.

I square my shoulders. "Save the Savior of the world or one small city?"

"Dear God!" Issaca breaths the words. Then shrugs. "Well, if it be that, you must go immediately!"

"But what about Grandfather? If they mean to –"

"I will take care of my husband! Go! Take your cousins, Nicias and Gaius with you. They are good men!"

"How will I find father? They've been gone a whole year!"

"Follow the Star like he did!" She grabs my arm. "But. Basil. When the Baby is safe, come home with all the speed you can muster!"

I give her a quick hug and head out the door.

꩜

I send Hammed to find Nicias and Gaius and go to the caravansary. They arrive as I'm supervising the preparations for the journey – three pack camels and three riding camels.

"Basil, we received your message. What's happening?" Nicias.

"The Child Father seeks in mortal danger!"

"How do you know?" Nicias.

"Ruby –"

"That stone again?" Scoffs Gaius.

"Yes, Gaius!" Dryly. "Will you go with me?"

"Of course!" Nicias, as both mount the waiting camels.

"Did you discuss this with Madjid?" Gaius asks as we leave the caravansary.

"With Issaca. She agrees that we must go."

Nothing more is said as we cross the Oxus River and head west and north into the hills surrounding the city of Bactra. The camels are fresh and happy to lope along at their mile-eating stride. We ride single file. I realize we cannot go further without them knowing what could be happening in Madjid. I stop and face them.

"What is it, Basil?" Gaius.

Chapter Nineteen - The Journey Begins

"Look! There's something else I need to tell you so you can decide. At the games I saw proof of plans to overthrow Madjid."

"We've heard a few rumors. But how you have proof!?" Gaius.

"Half of me wants you to stay and protect my grandfather, but the other half knows I need you with me."

Nicias and Gaius exchange glances.

"We ride with you, Basil!" Nicias. I nod, and we return to road.

"How can we possibly catch up with the Magi?" Gaius. "They've been gone a year or more."

"We'll exchange our Bactrian camels for Dromedaries in Bactra. They will do better in the desert than these mountain brutes."

"Ugh! Dromedaries! They smell funny, and they are so bad tempered!"

"They bite and spit!" Adds Gaius.

"They can go faster and further without water." I state firmly.

෮෴෮

Bactra sits in the hills west of the Oxus River. Hard riding gets us to the Caravansary by mid-afternoon and it takes some time and careful questioning and haggling to get a fair deal in trade for our Bactrian camels, but we finally succeed. We head out of the city and find a good place to camp for the night.

In the light of the campfire, I unroll one of Father's maps and trace the route I'd seen him mark out.

"Why did your father go north when the star is in the south-western sky?" Nicias.

"It's almost all desert due south and it's inhabited by hostile Assyrians. Father took the other Wise Men around it so we will follow him. We will be able to go much faster as we are only three and all mounted. I'm reckoning it will just take us a couple months to catch up with them."

Two of us settle into our rugs to sleep while the third stands watch. We will take turns through the night.

෮෴෮

The King is Born

We've been on the road for several days without incident, crossing the foothills of a mountain range and into the desert. It has rained here recently, and the desert spreads out before us carpeted with the red flowers that are here today and gone tomorrow.

The Greeks believe they are related to their god Adonis who was killed by the older god Ares. His blood spread across the desert and the red anemones appeared. Ever since then, when it rains the blood red flowers bloom. Unfortunately, the constant desert wind quickly rips off the petals and the plants die away.

"Basil! A storm is coming from the east!" Ruby has been silent for so long she startles me.

"Ruby! Um. Storms don't come from the east, Ruby."

"This is no ordinary storm, Basil! There is evil in it!"

I turn to look at the sky behind us where dark yellow-brown clouds billow. A flash of lighting briefly illuminates the malevolent face of Death.

"Sandstorm coming! Cover!" I shout as I leap off the camel and force both to kneel, facing away from the storm, and quickly tether them to stakes pounded into the sand. I drag out a canvas sheet. There's no time to stake it. I drop to the ground and roll up in it, pulling the edges closed around my head.

The sand hits, pelting the canvas with debris. The camels' grumbling grows louder, then quiets down. The weight on the canvas steadily increases, making it hard to breath. Finally, the wind dies down. I know to wait longer for the sand and dust to settle.

But all is too quiet.

"Ruby, what's happening?" I ask aloud.

"The storm is over. The evil is passed. You can free yourself now."

I struggle to push off the sand and unwrap myself. Two other mounds dissolve as Gaius and Nicias dig their own way out.

There's not a camel in sight!

"Oh no! We've lost the camels!" Cries Gaius.

"What should we do, Basil?" Nicias, uncertain.

"We'll have to find an oasis quickly to replenish our supplies and camels." I sigh.

CHAPTER NINETEEN - THE JOURNEY BEGINS

"Back in the higher hills there were more signs of water than out here. Perhaps we should backtrack a bit." Nicias. I shake my head.

"I want to keep moving forward. Surely, we'll find an oasis soon."

"Basil, he's right. We've been out here before in training exercises. There's no water in this stretch of desert."

"I've found some of your camels!" Ruby's voice is loud in excitement. *"They are in a gully just south of you."*

"We're in luck," I laugh and slap Gaius on the back. "That "stone" says they're close by in a sheltered gully!"

I unclasp Ruby's chain and hold her. She appears in one of her facets.

"The pack camels were young and untrained. They were so frightened. They pulled up their stakes and ran. The older camels followed, but stopped in the first shelter they found."

"Why didn't you tell me when it happened?"

"What could you have done? Evil was here. It would have taken you!"

"I beat him once before!"

"Twice, actually! But this time was different. Help will come soon. Until then you will manage."

"Thanks for the confidence! Wait what help?" Ruby fades out.

We find the three camels kneeling in the lee of an overhanging rock and mount them, encouraging them to get up. They grumble and spit, but do as we bid them. We ride back into the foothills searching for water.

Over the top of a ridge the tips of trees suggest there is water nearby. As if to confirm that, the camel's ears prick forward, and they begin to run up the ridge.

Topping it, we see the sun sparkling off a lake surrounded by Bedouin tents. Alerted by the sound of the running camels raises a shout from one of the camps. Men rush toward us, spreading out in front of their tents, shouting and pointing away from the oasis.

"They're waving swords at us, Basil!" Cries Nicias.

THE KING IS BORN

But the camels won't stop. They spit, kick and snap at the men trying to shoulder their way through the line of slashing swords. I jump down off my camel and raise my hands high and wide to protect my camel, but also to show we were not armed.

"We only want some water!" I shout. I mime drinking. But the Bedouin close ranks, the closest one a towered over me. A broad-shoulder brute with glittering black eyes beneath a chest long black mane. He steps in front of me, his legs apart, his arms folded across his chest, scimitar glinting in the sun.

I repeat my request in several different languages with miming.

The scimitar suddenly points forward and the giant steps closer so that its tip is just inches from my chest.

"I don't think they are going to let us near the water!" Nicias.

"Yah think?" Gaius. "Come on Basil before he runs you through!!"

The blade suddenly moves up Basil's chest toward Ruby, hooking her chain.

The sun catches in Ruby and flashes into the man's face. He shields his eyes.

Nicias urges his camel forward.

"Basil! Take my hand!"

Nicias grabs my raised arm and pulls me up onto his camel's neck. The slashing scimitar narrowly misses me. Gaius has caught the rains of my camel, and together, we make haste to depart the scene!

We return to the other side of the ridge, but the camels are still agitated and hard to control, the smell of water still in their nostrils. We keep moving up wind of the water until the camel's grumbling stops.

"Nicias, your camel's injured!" Gaius.

As Nicias stops the camel, I slide off inspect the camel as Nicias drops down to join me. We muzzle the camel and tie its reigns to a straggly thorn tree, allowing it to rest while I create a needle from one of the long thorns of the tree.

Chapter Nineteen - The Journey Begins

A camel's back kick can break a man's leg. We must be able to hobble it so I can stitch the cut which is on his left hindquarter.

Gaius grabs the reigns and wraps them around a stake he's pound in the ground, then passes the remainder to Nicias to secure on its other side. Gently, but firmly, they pull on the reigns until the camel's head is on the ground. Then they struggle to hobble the flailing legs.

The camel's cries are full of stress, bringing the other two to stand close to it, nuzzling its face. Their presence reassures the injured camel, and it settles.

Fortunately, I packed my medical kit on my camel and not on the pack camel. Even so, there's not much I can do, other than to wash the dirt and blood away and stitch the cut. The camel grumbles, his hindquarter shuddering with every prick. A couple times it tries to kick. But the job is quickly done. I dust it with some powder and step back.

In unison, we release him and jump back as it scrambles to its feet, kicking, bellowing and crying. The others comfort him, mumbling and nuzzling it.

"You can't ride him for a couple days, Nicias. We'll have to ride double."

"Nicias can ride with me for the rest of today. We can switch each day."

"Better get moving, then. We still need to find water." Nicias touches Gaius' shoulder in passing as he separates the camels.

We recross the Kopet Dag Mountains and head out into the Kavir Desert.

◈◈◈

It's hot. Oven hot. The sands shimmer, the hills looking like rolling waves on a vast sea.

Gaius is in the lead. Nicias and I ride together on the second camel, leading the injured one. Our pace is necessarily slow, not just for the injured camel, but because we need to find water. Camels can go days without water, because they store water in their humps. But their humps are empty and sagging beneath the saddles.

The King is Born

Gaius suddenly straightens in his saddle, shading his eyes with his hand.

"An oasis!" He shouts, pointing. "Thank the Mighty One!" He urges his camel forward and we follow. But the camels refuse to go faster and increase their grumbling, sounding more strident in their discomfort.

"Why won't they go faster? Can't they smell the water? I mean, a few days ago we couldn't stop them and now they don't seem at all interested."

"I don't know!" I shrug. "We can go faster on foot!"

We dismount and stake the camels together, then head for the oasis. But in the intense heat, it isn't long until we are exhausted. All three of us have stopped sweating. I feel as if my whole body is on fire.

We drop to the sand.

"How come the oasis looks no closer than it did when I first saw it?" Grumbles Gaius.

"Tell me what you see." Ruby.

"A lake. Palms. Maybe tents. The heat makes it hard to see."

"Basil, it sounds like a mirage!"

"What's a mirage?" I ask.

"It's an illusion caused by the sunlight on the rippling heated air as it rises."

"A mirage?" Gaius. "Ye gods! I've heard stories about them! You can chase them all day and never get to them. When the sun sets, they disappear. The gods created them to tease and torment humans!"

He and Nicias flop back on the hot sand. I sit staring at the beautiful sight until the sun sets, and the dark blanket of a moonless night slips in place.

"The moon's rising," Nicias mutters. "I could swear that's west!"

"There shouldn't be a moon tonight." I mutter, turning to see where he's pointing. "Let alone one rising in the west."

"Not the moon!" Gaius. "Too small."

Chapter Nineteen - The Journey Begins

I start laughing and can't stop, the laughter turning to dry sobs.

"It's the Star Father was following. Where we should be!" I groan in total despair.

The heat dissipates quickly, although the sand is still warm. We dig out sand to cover us, the lie down and pile it back on top. It will keep us warm at least for a while.

I'm in that halfway place between waking and sleeping when I hear Ruby.

"Basil, help is on the way."

"Am I dreaming or did Ruby just say...?"

Chapter Twenty
Help Arrives

I sit bolt upright, wide awake. Something –

"Camels are coming!" Ruby sounds excited.

"Camels? Our pack animals?"

"With riders on them!"

I shake the body next to mine.

"Shhhh! Ruby says riders are coming!"

Gaius shakes Nicias as I hear the jingle of metal.

In the bright starlight there is nowhere to hide. We crouch together, our short swords drawn.

Several riders emerge out of the gloom and stop at a little distance. The Lead man moves a little forward.

"I am looking for one who is called Basilikos, the grandson of Lady Issaca. Do you know of him? Have you seen him?"

"Who are you?" I ask.

The Leader laughs. "Basilikos! You saved my life! I am here to return the favor!"

"Thank the Mighty One!" I breath as the men dismount. The Leader dismounts and approaches holding out three water skins. We accept them greedily.

Belatedly I think of the camels and stop drinking.

"Our camels!" I cry.

"My men are caring for them." He gently takes the water skin from me. "Too much water, too quickly will make you sick!"

Confused and dazed, I turn to see a man placing hanging something above a fire. As the fragrance of roasting meat reaches me, my knees buckle. The Leader wraps an arm around my waist and leads me to a seat by the fire.

The King is Born

Gaius and Nicias are settled beside me in about the same state as I am.

The skewered meat is wrapped in flat bread and offered to us. I think I might have tasted the first bite, but the rest has gone down too fast. Flasks of water are handed out, and then dried dates. These I take my time over and enjoy what surly be the fruit of the gods!

While we were eating, the men had set up a Bedouin-style tent behind us. We are ushered into it and settle on bedrolls laid out on Persian rugs.

❦

I slowly wake and snuggle into a warm blanket.

"Was that a nightmare?" I open my eyes to see a canvas stretched above me.

"Canvas, not my ceiling. What's happened? Where am I?"

"A man named Mongke found you last night. He also rescued your camels." Ruby's familiar voice in my head is reassuring.

"Mongke? The name is familiar...He said that he was returning a favor - that I saved his life. The only man whose life I saved - we saved - was the one gored by a bull."

"The very one!"

"Ruby!" I am suddenly fully awake. Remembering the purpose for this trip. *"We need to get going! Father -"*

I throw back the blanket and scramble out of the tent in search of this Mongke fellow. I see him talking to another and hurry to him. He shakes hands with the man and turns to me, a welcome smile as he begins to speak. But I cut him off.

"Mongke, I must find my father and warn him! We need to get going immediately!"

"We will get going after you three have had a good meal." Mongke points to a low table laden with food.

"There's no time for that!" Panic sets in. "I must find Father! He's in danger and there's more danger back home as well. He doesn't know!" I grab his arm and shake it. In turn, he grips me by the shoulders and gives me a shake.

"Basilikos! Stop!" He waits for me as I gulp air trying to quell the panic.

Chapter Twenty - Help Arrives

"Ruby has told me about what you perceived after the games. She has also told me about the impression she has had that your father is in danger." He lets go of my shoulders. "First you eat, then we ride. Now sit!"

With child-like obedience, I sit. Nicias and Gaius join me and we tuck in to the food before us.

"I really want to get back on the road -" I hesitate. "But I still would like to know how you found us."

Mongke glances up and notices Ruby lying against my robe.

"Do you communicate with her?" He points to Ruby.

"Yes. It was Ruby who woke me as you approached."

"Then it is possible you might be able to accept my story." He glances at Nicias and Gaius.

"They're coming round." I grin.

"Very well. Five hundred years ago I was a brash and wild young man, hungry for action. I joined a cult - "

"Wait! Five hundred years ago? No one lives that long!" Nicias pauses with a hand half way to his mouth.

"There are many who have lived long lives. The Hebrew, Methuselah lived to be 969 years old." Mongke grins and continues. "This cult I joined had an initiation ceremony where, under a full moon, at the stroke of midnight, the initiate must slice the throat of a white bull. In my case, as I slit the bull's throat, it gored me. The cult members left my body beside the dead bull, and vanished into the night.

"Monks found me and took me to their monastery in the mountains. It was determined that there was no one who could save me, therefore I was taken to another realm to await the arrival of such a person."

"Another 'realm'." Gaius shakes his head.

"Do you believe in angels?" Mongke.

"Never seen one, but I've heard stories about them."

"Would you agree they are not of this world?"

"We're told they come from the Heavens, wherever they are." Gaius frowns.

THE KING IS BORN

"The word 'realm' is the same as the word 'heaven'."

Gaius nods. "Not much clearer, but, go on."

"I was taken to a realm where time does not exist, to wait for a human who could heal me."

"And that just happened to be me," I grin.

"You and Ruby."

"Yes, me and Ruby. Talk about trial by fire! I hadn't a clue what to do for you. Ruby helped. Evil and the bull that gored you were there. Evil wanted to take you. But Ruby –"

"It wasn't me!" Ruby interrupts. *"You called on the Most High God. He responded!"*

"That's right, Ruby. I did call on the Most High God and he responded with lighting and fire!" I suddenly remember something. "Mongke, you would know about the curse on the little guy who looked like a ram!"

"I do!" He chuckles. "He is my father. But that is a long story, too long for now. Let us get to the camels and ride!"

Chapter Twenty-One
Set Straight

❦❦

Once mounted, we ride four abreast with Nicias and Gaius taking the outside positions.

"All right, Mongke, time for you to tell us about this curse Basil broke!" Nicias.

"Very well. How much do you know about the first inhabitants of the plateau where Madjid stands?"

"We've heard part of it from our fathers. And Ruby has shared her memories up until she landed in the lake." I start. "Xanthos was beheaded, and Ruby landed in the lake."

"We've heard stories about the baby surviving and being raised by another tribe." Gaius.

"Xanthos had named the child Euphraino which translates Rejoice." Mongke begins. "He was sold to a childless couple of another tribe who had no knowledge where he came from. They named him Raamsal. He grew into a tall, handsome youth, much loved and admired by all his peers. He fell in love with the most beautiful girl in the country, and she with him. Her father was the High Priest of the temple, and in time, became a very powerful magician, delving into the Black Arts.

"Raamsal, who was destined to the priesthood, discovered that the High Priest was desecrating the temple with the Black Arts. He vowed to destroy him, even if it meant losing the woman he loved.

"The battle was ferocious! The only thing Raamsal had in his favor was his innocence. In the end, by a slight of hand which the High Priest had used moments before, Raamsal ran him through with his Scimitar.

With his dying breath the High Priest cursed Raamsal, using his own pride against him:

The King is Born

He would have the face and body of a ram, and live to be a thousand years old. And so, from that day on he was called Ramsskull."

"How strange!" Gaius. "That's what we called him because he never introduced himself!"

"You must have already been born, Mongke." I want to hear more, not reminisce.

"No. According to Father, she loved him so much that she claimed she never saw any difference in him. He was always the tall and handsome man with which she had fallen in love." He pauses. "She died in birthing me."

"I'm sorry!" My voice is low.

Mongke taps his camel. It breaks into its long-gated run, making conversation impossible. We follow.

❧

That evening when we stopped to rest, I urged Mongke to continue with the story. He obliged.

"After you and Ruby saved my life and broke the curse on Father, he lived a long and happy life. He married again and had many more children, one of which was the grandfather, many times removed, of your grandmother, Issaca." His demeanor suddenly changes, and he rises, dusting off his robes.

"We need to ride tonight! Come! Let us get on the way!"

I don't argue, as I had suddenly had an intense feeling of angst in my gut. Gaius and Nicias grumble a bit but follow us to the camels. We saddle them ourselves and head out, only half of Mongke's men with us.

We ride all through the night, heading west by south, and we do not stop when the sun rises.

For several days, the grueling pace continues until late one afternoon, we finally stop in the shade of a few scrawny trees of a small oasis.

It's hot. Flies buzz around us and we shoo them away with horsetails.

Mongke approaches, wiping his face with his sleeve.

"Basil, I have to leave you now."

Chapter twenty-One - Set Straight

"What? Why?" I rise to face him.

"I am leaving my men with you, plus four pack camels I just purchased from that vendor." He points across the water at one of the groups of tents there.

"Continue west by south until you reach Damascus. From there, follow the Star south."

"You aren't coming with us?" I suddenly feel very vulnerable, and try to think of something to keep him with us longer. "You don't want to see this child that Father says will change the world forever?"

"I have already met him." Mongke's face softens into a sweet smile has he grips my shoulder.

Instantly I see the laughing face of a little boy holding up his arms. Hands lift him –

The vision is gone. I look at Mongke. He nods and grins. "You are in for a wonderful treat!"

Chapter Twenty-Two
Finding Balthazar

We've been traveling nights as it's cooler and there's less traffic on the Roman roads. Once we reached Damascus, we did as Mongke said and followed the Star, taking local routes which are little more than beaten, dusty clay paths - hard to follow at night, had the light from the Star not been bright enough to see the way.

We did return to the Roman road that goes around the Sea of Galilee, over the hills of Samaria, to Joppa, on the coast. From there we've been traveling a wide path east by south-east, but through the hills of Judea, heading for Jerusalem.

As the sun rises, Nicias points at a high wall with rows of roofs flowing away behind it.

"Jerusalem?"

"It must be!" Gaius, the excitement in his voice is contagious. "Look at the line of people waiting to enter the gates!"

One of Mongke's men stops beside me. "Sir, it would be best to set up camp out here where others are already. Once you have had time to clean up and rest you can enter the city and search for your father."

"It's taken several months for us to get here. No telling what's already happened back home! I need to get to my father!" I turn to look at him. He raises one eyebrow and cocks his head. "You know something!"

"No, sir. It would be what Mongke would do. Dusty and tired, you are at a disadvantage. Camping out here and speaking with some of the others who are here -" He points to a large spread of tents. "You might learn more about current events."

"Very well," I sigh. "Gaius, Nicias, we'll stop here and set up camp, clean up and enter the city later this afternoon." They nod in agreement.

The King is Born

We start toward a place by a stream that had recently been vacated.

"Master Basilikos?" I glance at my cousins, then turn to look at the men behind me. "Master Basilikos!" A man is running alongside my camel waving at me. I do a classic double take, frowning. I know him.

"Josias?" I cry, pulling my camel to a stop and dropping off its back to hug my father's personal servant. "Where's Father? I must speak to him immediately!"

My cousins are instantly beside me. I pass off the camel's reigns to someone and follow Josias in amongst the large caravan we'd noticed at first. Josias stops beside one of the tents and raises his hand, his finger to his lips. His eyes are sparkling, his lips curved in a grin.

He steps around the corner of the tent and, trying to speak normally, he says, "My Lord Balthazar, I have a wonderful surprise for you!"

"What, more good news, Josias?"

I take a deep breath and pause for a moment. It's good to hear my father's voice, gentle as always. But it won't be like that for long. I step around the tent pole and stand beside Josias.

As I knew it would, the pleasant expression on his face dissolves, his lips forming a grim line as he rises from the low table before him.

"Basilikos! What are you doing here? Why have you left Madjid alone?"

"Two reasons, Father." I speak through clenched teeth to keep them from clicking together. "First, you and the child you seek are in mortal danger!"

Cheng Sherong and Gandophares rise and join us.

"What makes you say that?" Cheng Sherong.

"Ruby warned me while I was still in Madjid."

Father snorts. "You mean the gemstone, the ruby? Warned you! You're as crazy as Mother!"

"And Issaca told me to come to warn you of that and -"

Chapter Twenty-Two - Finding Balthazar

"You left an old woman to fight twelve of my brothers and their fathers?" He swivels and heads for another tent, his fists clenched, his back rigid.

"There's more!" I shout after him. He keeps walking. I catch up with him and grab his arm, trying not to cringe at the anger mottling his face.

"Issaca said to be quick about what you have to do here and hurry home as fast as you can. There is danger brewing at home as well!"

"AND STILL YOU LEFT!" I let go his arm, my courage pouring away like water.

"Listen to him, Balthazar!" Gandophares and the others now surround us.

"Speak!" Father spits the word at me.

"At the end of the games. I beat Cyrus in the final round. " His eyebrows shoot up and some of the anger subsides. He offers me his hand. I take it and continue, "I ... I ... I saw a vision." I say it quickly because I know he might scoff again. But he nodded, instead.

"I saw the walled city of Madjid shrouded in a gray cloud, the fields barren, the orchards dead. Cyrus, dressed as the Army Commander rode through the city gates ahead of a full army that spread out, barring the way for your returning caravan."

Father's face pales, his expression turning to anguish. In the silence, the sounds around us are loud.

"My Father? Mother?"

"I didn't get to see what had or was happening inside. I'm sorry, Father. Truly, I am. When I told Issaca, she immediately commanded me to come and tell you."

No one speaks or moves for a full minute. Cheng Sherong lays his hand on Father's shoulder, "Let us get out of this sun and return to the tent. We can continue this discussion there."

We do as he suggests, grateful for a little relief from the glare and heat. As we accept drinks from Josias, Cheng Sherong takes the lead.

"We arrived the night before last. Yesterday, Josias went to the king to request a visit with him. We are scheduled for tomorrow.

The King is Born

He did came back, though, with a gold mine of information." He turns to Josias, who has joined us on the cushions.

"It wasn't long after the three Magi retired that we were visited by several elders of the city." I listen to Josias, seeing in my mind what had happened.

☙❦❧

Josias ushers the elders into the tent in which we now sit. As they settle, Josias makes father's apologies, speaking in Greek.

"My Lords, please forgive my Master for not receiving you," Josias serves them refreshments. "We have traveled all night, and he has retired to his tent."

"Who is your master?" One asks, looking around at the luxury of the expansive tent.

"My Master is Magus Balthazar son of Madjid Jenghiz, Counselor to the Patriarch, and High Priest at the temple in the city of Madjid. The others are Magus Gandophares from India and Magus Cheng Sherong from China." The elders nod wisely. "Madjid is a mighty walled city in the country of Bactria on the north-western side of the Himalayan Mountains. It has taken us almost two years to travel here," explains Josias. "My Master has come to pay homage to the newborn King of the Jews."

The elders whisper amongst themselves before responding to this news.

"We already have a King. King Herod was appointed by Rome and as far as we know, none of his wives have given birth recently." They are cautious. "Perhaps your Master should speak to King Herod."

"That would be the thing to do," Josias bows in acknowledgment. "If you will give me directions, I will go immediately to make an appointment for my Master with King Herod."

"We will take you there ourselves." They all nod in agreement.

As they are leaving the camp, Josias stops to talk to another servant, speaking in a language the elders did not recognize.

"Forgive me, my lords, my Master would be furious if I did not let him know where I was going."

Chapter Twenty-Two - Finding Balthazar

Once in the palace, Josias is led to the King's secretary to make an appointment. But when he hears the nature of their mission, the secretary's guarded expression creases with worry lines. He excuses himself, hurrying away.

After a rather long wait, he returns and, wringing his hands, tells Josias that the King will speak with him. Josias follows him into the King's Chamber.

The King is less than pleased when Josias confirms that the Wise Men are here to pay homage to the newborn King of the Jews. As Josias is ushered out of the hall, several men hurry in. From their apparel I assume these are the Pharisees, Sadducees, Scribes and more.

The shadows have moved again before Josias is called back in and told to bring the Magi in the next day. And he's abruptly dismissed. As he is leaving, those around the king all begin talking at once. Josias walks slowly to the door, listening as long as he can.

"Make sure your Masters discuss this with no one until I see them! Do you understand?" Herod's voice carries above the chatter around him. Josias bows and turns to leave as Herod drops his voice to speak to those around him.

✧✦✧

"And what did you manage to understand from the argument?" I interrupt, not having been listening to what he was saying. Josias pauses. I realize I've interrupted him in mid-sentence. "I'm sorry, I interrupted you, Josias!"

"I was just going to tell you, sir. They were asking each other what this was all about: Was it is a plot by the Romans to see how loyal they are? Was it the rabble-rouser whom they had recently arrested? Oh, yes, the last thing I heard was King Herod ordering the scribes to bring in the scrolls."

Cheng Sherong sits forward. "This is an interesting turn of events, isn't it?"

"I suggest we return to the translation of the scrolls we received yesterday," Father moves to a table littered with scrolls and manuscripts.

✧✦✧

Chapter Twenty-Three
Some Discoveries

꩜

We spend the rest of the morning reading, translating and discussing different scrolls and manuscripts that the Magi had brought with them. At noon we take a break for a meal. The talk turns to how to approach a baby king and what gifts to present to him.

"I'm presenting him with a crown of gold," says Gandophares. It's the right gift for a king."

"I bring him Frankincense," Cheng Sherong. "It owns its own deity, being a precious oil used in the very finest of perfumes. In powdered form, we use it to scent the trunks in which we store fine linens and clothing. Its fragrance is unparalleled. And, if you take the sawdust and the shavings from the wood itself and put them on the coals, its aroma is matchless. It is the only incense worthy of a king."

"I'm familiar with Frankincense," I but in. "It's used by the High Priest to lift the prayers of the people into the presence of the Highest God. It is a gift worthy of a High Priest!" I turn to Balthazar, waiting for him to share what gift he brings. But he stays silent, so I push. "What gift do you bring, Father?"

"Myrrh," slightly hesitant.

"Myrrh!" I study his face and see that he also questions his gift. "Father, why myrrh? I know we use it in the temple along with the frankincense both as incense and in the anointing oil.

"And I know from Issaca that it has many uses in medicines, especially for woman's ailments. But it is also one of the main ingredients that the embalmers use to mummify the body of a king or priest after death!"

"That is true, my son."

"What then? Incense, anointing oil or embalming aide?"

The King is Born

"Some things are hard to understand, Basilikos," Gandophares begins. "We will try to explain to you just what we've discovered. As you know, we've been studying many old manuscripts: the writings of the Prophet Zoroaster, the stories of the Chinese, some from the Babylonians, the Greeks, the Medes and others. And most recently, the writings of the Israelites. All of them say that a superior Star will appear heralding the birth of a very special person - a king of sorts.

"The Israelite manuscripts are more specific." Father takes over. "They say that this person will be of the lineage of their King David. They say that he will reign wisely and do what is just and right in the land. The Spirit of the Israelite's god will be upon him, making him wise, understanding and compassionate, and because of that, able to give good counsel. He will be full of power and knowledge and the fear of their god."

"Why do you look for him now, as a baby? Why not just wait until he comes into his kingdom?"

"It is very important that we pay homage to this king now. By doing so, we hope to make good alliances between our countries – if he truly is to rule the world," explains Gandophares. "The Babylonians, Romans and Greeks have many gods each. We who follow the teachings of the Prophet Zarathustra believe in one God, Ahura Mazda, the Wise Lord, who is the sole Creator and Lord of the world. The seven Amesha Spentas, or Bountiful Immortals, are divine beings who act as agents of the power of Ahura Mazda."

I glance at Cheng Sherong. "You seem doubtful, Magus Sherong. Almost skeptical about all of this."

"I am, to a point. What Gandophares says it is similar to the religions of my people. There's good and evil in all things – the yin and the yang – and there are gods that rule each. It is a constant battle."

"But according to the writings of Zarathustra," I wish to show some knowledge. "Ahura Mazda has decreed that truth will triumph in the end."

"These Israelites have only one god, also," Father breaks in. "But they believe that their god is the only god, the One True God. They deny the existence of any other gods."

Chapter Twenty-Three - Some Discoveries

"Can this be possible?" I question. "I've heard some of the Israelites as they have spoken with Father. Is it possible that their god really is the one and only true God?"

"Why, Basilikos," asks Gandophares. "What makes them so special? Why should their god be the One True God and not yours? Besides, how can there be only one God? You've watched your Grandfather and your Father as they have run the daily affairs of just one city. Can you imagine how mighty a single deity would have to be to run the affairs and control the daily lives of the entire world? No. It's easier for our minds to imagine that there are many gods, each with his particular principality to govern."

"Then you don't believe the teachings of Zarathustra? That there is only one God."

"No, I don't!" Gandophares emphatically. "At least, not entirely. Besides, if the Israelite's god is the One True God and if He is so mighty and if these people are the "chosen" race, why are the Israelites a conquered people?"

"Exactly!" Cheng Sherong agrees. "If this god of theirs is so mighty, why was their country over run and why were they sold into slavery more than once?"

"Perhaps this king is going to overthrow the Roman government and free his people?" I muse. "But, will he stop there, or will he continue until he rules the whole world? And how will that make him any different from any other tyrant that has ruled before him?"

"From the writings that I have read," Father. "This god of theirs, when he made the earth, set it in motion with all the laws of good and evil, action and reaction - consequences, if you will. In their writings this god warns them about these laws, telling the people how to make the laws work for their own good, but they constantly ignored his warnings and went about doing whatever it was that pleased them. So, the consequences of the law finally caught up with them. They were weakened by their own immorality and, when the enemies came in like a flood, they were easy prey."

"The Prophet Zarathustra states that there has always been a battle between good and evil" Gandophares continues the thought. "Ahura Mazda, whom we believe to be the Supreme

The King is Born

Being, created both Ormazd, Lord of Light and Good and Ahriman, Lord of darkness and evil. Ormazd then created the material and spiritual world. But in retaliation, Ahriman called into being an opposing world."

"According to the Torah," Father continues. "Which is the oral and written records of the Israelites, their god, for whom they have many names: El Elyon, the Most High God; El Shaddai, the Almighty God, and Yahweh, meaning Redeemer, to name just a few. Yahweh, the most commonly used, made the earth out of nothing. But instead of 3,000 years, He made it in only seven days, creating the land and the water and all living creatures. Last of all He created man in male and female form and put them in a garden to enjoy it and to tend it. But the evil one came in as a cunning serpent and deceived the female and the corruption of the world began. At that time, Yahweh prophesied to Satan, the evil one who came in the form of a serpent, that there was One coming whose heel he - Satan - would bruise, but who would, in the end, crush his head."

"I do see some similarities to Zarathustra's writings," I said. "But, where did the evil one come from, according to the Torah?"

"I don't know," Father shakes his head.

"Who is the one who will crush his head?"

"Perhaps it is this one who is born right now?" Gandophares.

"And so, my question still stands," I interject, after a long silence. "Is this king going to free his people now? Will he attempt to conquer the whole world? And will he be any different from any other tyrant that has ruled before him?"

"I don't know that either," admits Father. "Isaiah is one of their chief prophets. He says that this king will re-establish the throne of David, one of their greatest kings. How, I do not know. And, that this kingdom will have no end. The Messiah, the one for whom all the Israelites wait, is supposed to come and do many wonderful things: healing the sick, opening blind eyes, making the lame to walk again, releasing captives and re-establishing that mighty kingdom.

"However," He puts up a hand to stop me from interrupting him. "Isaiah says that he will be accused of doing evil and will be abused by the people. He will not defend himself. He will be as silent

Chapter Twenty-Three - Some Discoveries

as a lamb being led to the slaughter. He will allow them to kill him because of the wrongs of the people, not because of what he did. Then he will be buried in a grave with the wicked, as if he were a violent man, when, in truth, he never even told a lie."

"So! This is why you bring him myrrh!" It's a statement, not a question. After another long silence, I continue. "It doesn't make much sense. First of all, you say his kingdom will last forever. Then you say he's going to be killed.

"So, if he's going to be cut down in his prime, why try to establish relations with him now? . . . And why the lamb comparison?"

"I can answer your question about the lamb," Cheng Sherong. "The Israelites offer a sacrificial lamb once a year as a sin offering to their god. The blood of that lamb covers the sins that they committed during the year. That lamb must be spotless, without blemish of any kind." After a moment, he adds, "The Israelites have many ritualistic sacrifices. Their religion is very strict on what they can and cannot do. Ours is a much simpler practice."

"Isaiah calls this man 'The Lamb of God' because he will be pure, without spot or blemish, just like that sacrificial lamb Cheng Sherong spoke of," Father returns to my question. "He never will have sinned or in any way have displeased their god, therefore, he will be acceptable as their final sacrifice - their guilt offering, and he will replace the lamb that they sacrifice at Passover each year. Isaiah said he is the Messiah, the Christ, the Anointed One - the One Chosen of God for this purpose."

"So, he's going to die for the people," I said. "But, again: if he dies, how can his kingdom be without end?"

"That is, indeed, a good question, Basilikos, and one I asked and still ask." Gandophares interjects. "The parchments your Father acquired from the Israelites have shed some light on all of this."

Shaking his head, Cheng Sherong repeats. "Much of it is hard to understand, let alone believe!"

"According to this Isaiah," Father begins. "Even though their God allows this Messiah to be killed, He will raise him up again and will give him a place among the great. In the songs your mother sings, those written by the Israelite King David, it says that their

The King is Born

god has even made him to sit at god's own right hand until all his enemies have been made his footstool! It is just possible that his kingdom will last forever."

"This is getting metaphysical!" I feel a thrill run through my body "I believe you're getting into the spirit world, Father. We know that God, by whatever name you wish to call him, is a Spiritual Being. If this man is to sit on the right hand of God, his kingdom must be a spiritual kingdom. So why are you comparing it to a physical kingdom? In fact, is he really a man at all?"

"Are you suggesting that this man is a result of a union between a spiritual being and a human?!" Gandophares splutters. "It's true that we believe this has happened in the past - the giants of the Philistines and the horribly disfigured creatures of the night. no! No! NO! This man must be different!"

"Basilikos!" Father cautioned. "This talk is not good. We are getting into things we know nothing about. Stop now."

As the sun sets, I glance up at the stars, noticing our Star. But it's not where I expect it to be!

"Look, Father!" I exclaim, pointing to it.

"Would you look at that!" Exclaims Cheng Sherong.

"Did any one notice where the Star was last thing this morning?" Gandophares looks around the circle of faces.

"No, I confess I didn't pay any attention," admits Father. "I assumed it would be over the palace."

"If I may speak, my Lord," says Josias who has come to light torches for us.

"Yes, Josias, what is it?"

"The last time we saw the Star was as we were coming over the rise into the Kidron Valley. The Star was to the southwest, but so was Jerusalem. By the time we began setting up camp, the sun was well up, and the Star was gone."

"So it was," agrees Father. "Well, if this child was not born in Jerusalem, where else do you think he could have been born?" He turns back to the rest of us.

"I read something this afternoon that might tell us," I reach for the scroll that I had been reading.

Chapter Twenty-Three - Some Discoveries

"Josias, bring me one of those torches. It's hard enough to translate this stuff without doing it in the dark!"

"What have you found?" The others crowd around me, Josias, too.

"You have been studying Isaiah, Father, but this scroll that you gave me to translate was written by one of the lesser prophets, Micah. This is what I've translated: 'But you, O Bethlehem Ephrathah, are only a small village among all the people of Judah. Yet a ruler of Israel, whose origins are in the distant past, will come from you on my behalf.'[1]"

But you, Bethlehem Ephratah, though you are only a small village among the people of Judah. On My behalf, out of you shall come a Ruler of Israel, Whose origins are from long ago."

"My Lord?" Josias speaks again.

"Please, Josias, let's not stand on ceremony now!" Father, irritation sounding in his voice. "You're as much a part of this as any of us!"

"Thank you, my Lord. You were thinking that Jerusalem is the City of David and, so it is. Originally it was Zion, the fortified city of the Jebusites. King David captured it and called it the City of David. In fact," his voice warming to the chance to talk of his homeland. "It was through a tunnel from this very Spring of Gihon that Joab crawled to break through the fortress."

"Really! That's very interesting, Josias," Father's voice doesn't sound all that interested. "So, you are saying that there is another city called the City of David?"

"Yes, my Lord. This Bethlehem that Master Basilikos just read about is also called the City of David, because he was born there."

Father picks up the scroll he had been studying. "Isaiah says, there shall come forth a rod out of the stem of Jesse, and a Branch shall grow out of his roots: And the spirit of the Lord shall rest upon him.[1]"

"That makes sense, my Lord," Josias, eagerly. "Jesse was the father of King David and King David was born in this town, Bethlehem of Judea."

---

[1] Isaiah 11:1-2, King James Version of the Bible

THE KING IS BORN

"That is interesting!" I emphasize the "is".

"What is?" Asks Father.

"What you just read. A Branch shall grow out of his roots. Use grapevines for example. You cut it down completely and you think you have killed it, but when you least expect it, a shoot appears, and the vine grows back, sometimes healthier and stronger than the original plant."

"After all these years without a true leader, Israel has seemed to be dead. A people without hope. And now, in their darkest hour, when he is least expected, a leader appears and restores the kingdom?" Muses Father.

"Where is this Bethlehem from here?" Asks Gandophares.

"About five miles due south, my Lord," Josias.

We turn in unison to look for the Star. It hangs low over the hills -

Due south.

Chapter Twenty-Four
Good News

Later that evening, Father, Cheng Sherong, and Gandophares are lounging and talking outside of Father's tent. The subject has not changed.

I had disappeared soon after our discovery of the Star's appearance and am still not back. Father hadn't been too worried because I had taken Josias with me, but now it's past midnight.

"Good evening, Father," I call as I stride out of the darkness, Josias at my side.

"Basilikos!" The relief sounds in Father's voice.

"I'm sorry I am so late, but when you hear what I've learned, I believe you will be as excited as I am," I step aside to let Father see that several rough looking men have accompanied me. "I met these shepherds." Father rises and bows to the men. Gandophares and Cheng Sherong do the same.

"Please, come and sit by our fire and warm yourself, the night is chilled," Father offers them cushions. "May I offer you something to eat and drink, my lords?"

"My Lord, we are but lowly shepherds, we do not deserve to eat and drink with you." Father bows his head in acknowledgment.

"I am learning," he speaks slowly, with consideration. "That rank and title do not necessarily mean one is better than another. Please, you have obviously walked hard and fast to bring us your news. Josias will be glad to prepare the proper food and drink for you."

"Thank you, my lord. We accept your hospitality."

"Good! Josias?" But Josias has already left.

"Father," I could not hold still any longer. "You must hear what these men have to say!" Father glances at me.

The King is Born

Custom demands that we wait until our guests had eaten before discussing business.

"Forgive the exuberance of my son," he apologizes, bowing once again to the shepherds. "We have come a long way on a rather strange mission. I am afraid we are completely consumed with it."

"That is all right, my lord. Your son has told us that you follow the Star and are seeking the Baby King." He glances around, then lowers his voice, "We've seen Him!"

It is a comic moment that I shall remember always. Gandophares is reaching for something, Cheng Sherong is adjusting his robes, and Father is about to sit down. At the shepherd's whisper, they freeze in place – well, Father completely misses the pillows, but no one else notices as they speak at once.

"You've seen him? You've actually seen him?"

"Where did you find him?"

"How did you know?"

"They'll answer all your questions," I laugh with glee, grabbing Father's hand to pull him up. "If you give them a chance!" I turn to the shepherds. "I told you they'd be excited!"

"Forgive us!" Father cries. "Basilikos is right, we are very excited. My servant went to Herod yesterday asking about the baby. He didn't seem to know anything about him. In fact, he seemed very suspicious. We have an audience with him tomorrow at noon."

"He would not know anything about him," one of the shepherds replies. "The Baby was not born in his palace - or any palace for that matter."

"Not born in a palace! Then where was he born?"

"In a stable."

"In a stable?"

"Yes, my lords."

"Please! Please! Tell us your story!" Demands Cheng Sherong.

"Well, my lord, it was during the winter of last year. We had the sheep down on the lower hills to pasture. It was late at night; the sheep were all corralled and peaceful."

Another picks up the story.

Chapter Twenty-Four - Good News

"We were dozing by the fire, when suddenly there was a Person standing in front of us. Not just an ordinary man, for he was dressed in a robe of pure white and he was surrounded by a light as bright as the sun itself!"

"An angel of the Lord! I have read in your scriptures about such appearances. Did it frighten you?" Asks Father, in awe.

"We were terrified!"

"But the Angel immediately told us not to be afraid, that he brought us good news of such great joy that it would affect all the people of the world!"

"You could feel and see the Angel's excitement," adds a shepherd boy. "He trembled and shook, almost as badly as we did!" The men chuckle as his father nudges him to be quiet.

"What was his good news?"

"He said that on that day, in the City of David, a Savior was born. He said that this child was the Anointed One of God, chosen to be our Savior. Then he said that we would find this child in a manger."

"Before we could get our wits about us, the heavens burst open filled with angels! They were praising God and singing with such joy! Each one was singing their own song, but as we listened, it all seemed to come together, and we could understand their words clearly. Their message was this: 'Glory to God in the Highest. Peace on earth. Good will toward men!' It was truly a breathtaking sight!"

"And, as suddenly as they had appeared, they were gone. The sky was black, but it was not silent - we could still hear the angels singing. The stars shimmered as if they, too, were singing. After a long time, we began to talk in whispers. Finally, we decided to go to Bethlehem and see if we could find this child."

"And you did. In a stable, just like the angel said!" I almost shout it with excitement.

"Yes, my Lord. In a stable, for there was no room in the inns."

"Why was there no room in the inns?"

"The Romans had called for a complete census of our people, for tax purposes. They demanded that everyone return to their birthplace and stay there until the census was over."

The King is Born

"So, all the inns and public houses were full. None of the innkeepers would let them in, even though the woman was heavy with child!"

"I've heard of this census," Gandophares nods. "But what I don't understand is why they would not make room for a king. And what king comes from Bethlehem? Herod is an Edomite."

"I do not know, my Lords, I am only a shepherd. I am not learned in the Scriptures. Perhaps you should ask a Scribe. They would know these things." After a moment, he adds, "but the Baby's parents are not royalty. His father is a simple carpenter from Nazareth."

"This mystery gets even deeper. Perhaps talking with a Scribe would be the best thing to do. When we meet with Herod tomorrow, he may have already found out for us. Now, please, Josias has brought some food for you. Eat and drink and rest." The shepherds comply, answering questions as they can, then excusing themselves, they leave to return to their sheep.

"Balthazar, you've been quiet for some time now. What's going through your mind?" Asks Gandophares.

"The passage Basilikos translated earlier tells us he would be born in Bethlehem. And he is of the lineage of David, not Herod. His parents were not royalty, but lowly people - a carpenter, the shepherd said. That is why they were not recognized and given preferential treatment. He was born in a stable. Why? Why was he not recognized by his own people? Why weren't they looking for him? Weren't they curious about the Star? I mean, if you had a star like that hanging in the sky over your head, wouldn't you go looking to see what it was about? And did no one else hear and see the host of angels? And if not, why the shepherds? I need to think!"

In frustration, he gets up and leaves the tent.

Chapter Twenty-Five
Visiting Herod

༺♥༻

The morning is warm, with a soft breeze blowing up the valley, carrying with it the dissipating smoke from smoldering cooking fires. The servants are busy about their morning tasks, laughing and talking as they go.

Cheng Sherong, Gandophares and I lounge outside Father's tent. It is well into mid-morning before Father joins us. He is wearing a fresh tunic and robe, and his step is brisk. Only the fine lines around his eyes and the crease in his brow betray the lack of sleep and the long hours studying.

"Good morning, Magus Balthazar," greets Gandophares. "What did you find out? What conclusions did you reach last night?"

"It's amazing how quiet it is in the night watch," said Father. "I did a lot of thinking, trying to put things in order."

"All right," Cheng Sherong. "Tell us what you've sorted out."

"I began with what we agreed is true - our own manuscripts and writings from our own prophets, then the prophets of Baal, Greece and Persia, then added to that what we've learned from the Hebrew scrolls. It is prophesied that the religious men of this land were not be aware and ready for their king. They say that the people will not recognize him, from his birth even to his death. They say that he won't dress as a king, live as a king, nor in any way behave as a king. In other words, his clothing will be simple, he will have nowhere to call his own and he will eat and drink with the commoners."

"It doesn't sound much like a king, to me," Cheng Sherong.

"The Israelites are plagued with rebels and zealots who plot to overthrow the current government. It seems to me that, if he dresses and behaves as you've described, he'll be mistaken for one of these," Gandophares.

The King is Born

"In fact," continues Father. "That is what is going to happen. That is why we brought the gifts we did. The gold and frankincense for his kingship, but the myrrh for his burial. We talked about this before."

"Then, I must ask it again," I demand. "If he is going to be cut off in his prime, before he even establishes his kingdom, why are we here?" There is no answer to this and we sit in silence.

"My Lords, forgive me for interrupting," it's Josias. Out of habit, he waits for permission to continue. "I have been thinking, my Lords. I believe that it would be wise for you to present yourselves to King Herod in all the state and pomp that we can muster."

"I trust you Josias, for you are one of these people. We will do as you suggest. But what is your reasoning?"

"My Lord, I am not sure I can explain it. Maybe just a feeling?"

"You've worked too long for Balthazar and Basilikos!" Chuckles Gandophares. "If we're going to put on our full regalia, we'd better get going!"

"Josias, can you find someone to help Basilikos? He didn't think to bring his personal servant with him. Then come to me as quickly as you can," Father is already on the move.

"Already done, my Lord," Josias turns to a young man standing behind him. "Master Basilikos, you know Jonathan. He will assist you. Your clothes have already been laid out."

Yes, I know Jonathan. He's a cousin. A little awkward that he should be helping me dress.

The clothing is my father's and, although he is much larger than I, Jonathan quickly makes it fit with a tuck here and a twist there.

"Hold still. You fidget worse than a girl."

"You should have more respect!"

"I should. There! That is the best I can do. But without a beard you look way too young." He stood back to look me over. "Yes, you are the son of a Magus." He bows and stands aside for me to leave the tent.

Chapter Twenty-five - Visiting Herod

The camels are ready and adorned with every bit of finery Josias could find. On each camel's back is a howdah – a chair with an awning above it and shades that can be drawn for privacy. It's big enough to stretch out and take a nap on long journeys. The awnings are red and gold brocade, with tassels and little bells hanging from their rims. Behind our camels came several Bactrian camels, their long black hair brushed until it shines as it floats in the breeze. Each is loaded with gifts for Herod and decked out with more bells and tassels.

The spectacular entourage quickly draws attention. The two-humped Bactrian camels alone, draw attention, their flowing hair making the ungainly stride of the huge beasts seem graceful. Horse-mounted guards ride alongside us and the pack animals.

By the time we reach Herod's Palace, we have drawn quite a crowd. As camels do, ours protested loudly when commanded to kneel for us to disembark. The children in the crowd enjoy the sounds, giggling and pointing.

We enter the mighty Hall of King Herod, Father leading the way. From his shoulders swings the blue cape of the Magus. Under this he wears a voluminous purple robe fringed with gold braid. Under the robe he wears a loose-fitting white linen tunic that comes to his knees. Beneath the tunic are full linen pantaloons tied at his ankles. On his feet are simple black silk slippers. On his head sits a gold silk skullcap with a tall golden spike. Around this a pure white turban is wound, intertwined with gold braids. On his fingers and around his neck gold glitters and shimmers, encrusted with precious gems. His bearing is regal, his presence overwhelming.

To Father's right is Gandophares. The heavy blue cape, clasped with gold broaches, is thrown back over his shoulders. The lines of his white tunic and straight-legged trousers are simple, but elegant in their simplicity. Made of silk embroidered with gold and silver, the fabric moves and breaths with him. Gold slippers cover his feet. A gold fez sits on his head. He also wore several rings and gold necklaces. His bearing is also regal, but his presence only shimmers in Father's shadow.

Beside Gandophares strides Cheng Sherong, the blue cape, clasped at his shoulders, swings majestically with each step. A black silk tunic beneath it is open to the waist exposing his broad, hairless,

The King is Born

tanned chest. His legs are draped in black silk tied at the knees. His calves are bare, as are his feet. His head is shaved, except for a braid wrapped with gold hanging down his back. Around his neck and down his chest, gold glitters. He walks with his feet apart, his fists on his hips, holding back the blue cape to reveal his magnificent physique.

I walk on the other side of Father, holding my head high, my shoulders back. I am dressed in tunic and pantaloons, my robe, a simpler affair to Father's, is of purple silk, trimmed with gold. The blue cape of the Magi also hangs from my shoulders. My only piece of jewelry is Ruby. She shimmers on my young chest with every beat of my own heart.

At the other end of the great hall, Herod sits on his throne. Emulating the great Caesar in his posture, he leans back to one side, his elbow on the armrest, his chin on his fist. His other arm dangles limply over the armrest. His knees are spread, his heels tucked back against the chair. Around him the Pharisees and the Sadducees huddle, behind them, a contingency from Rome stands on guard.

"Your Royal Highness, King Herod," Father says, stepping forward and bowing. We also bow in obeisance to Herod. "We are honored to be in your presence today. I am Magus Balthazar, son of Madjid, of the Clan of Madjid." He bows again, then turns to Gandophares who steps forward.

"I am Magus Gandophares of India." He bows with a sweep of his arm.

Cheng Sherong takes a stance, feet apart, fists still on his hips. "I am Magus Cheng Sherong from China." He bows with a sweep of his right arm, palm open.

Father turns to me. I step forward and bow.

"I am Basilikos, Son of Balthazar, of the Clan of Madjid."

"My Lords!" Herod's tone matches his posture. I wonder if the boredom is put on for us, or if he really is so bored with life. "Welcome to Jerusalem." He makes a circular motion with the hand dangling over the arm of his chair but doesn't disturb his relaxed posture. I find myself irritated with his behavior, until I suddenly realize that he is intently studying us, taking in the magnificence of our robes and the chests the servants are carrying forward.

Chapter Twenty-five - Visiting Herod

"I understand that you are astrologers, magicians and sorcerers and that you interpret dreams." His eyes sharpen. "What brings you to Jerusalem?"

"My Lord, King," I sense Father's struggle to keep civil. "We do study the stars and on occasion, we have been able to interpret dreams. But we are not sorcerers or magicians. We are simply learned men, priests of the temple of our peoples. We have brought gifts for you from our countries as a token of honor and respect. If I may, my Lord," He claps his hands, and the servants begin to open the chests they carry. "We present to you, rare spices from India, your Highness. Fabrics made of the finest Chinese silks. Persian rugs of a magnificence unrivaled anywhere. Rare gems set in fine gold and silver to grace the necks of your fairest wives. Perfumed oils to soften their skin and make their hair shine." Herod bows his head in acknowledgment.

The men around the throne try hard to act as though they, too, are not in the least interested, but as the gifts are set before the king, as the silks billow down the steps, as the perfumes fill the air with their sweetness, they begin to murmur among themselves. Herod holds up his hand to silence them.

"Thank you, my Lords. I am sure my wives will appreciate your gifts," languidly, once again gesticulating with the limp wrist dangling over the arm of his chair. "These are truly magnificent gifts. I accept them as a token of friendship between our countries." He finally moves, getting up from the throne, he walks toward us. "Now, let us enjoy some fine food and entertainment." We follow him down a hall to a massive Banqueting room.

༺♥༻

The feasting and entertainment continue all through the afternoon and late into the evening. Nothing is said that would even hint at Herod's knowing why we are here. We wait. It is a game that must be played, and, for now, time is still on our side.

As midnight approaches, Father glances at me. I have been staring into the flames of a brazier for some time. Beads of perspiration have formed on my upper lip and my face has lost all color. Herod notices me, too.

The King is Born

"Is he seeing visions?" He asks Father as he sucks greedily from his goblet.

"No, my Lord," Father smiles as an indulgent father might. "Basilikos is young. He is not used to such magnificent celebrations. I believe that he is just very tired and about to fall asleep." At his words, I close my eyes and slip down on my couch released into sleep. The older men laughed and reminisced about their youth.

Then Herod makes his move.

"So," he says. "You have come to pay homage to a newborn King of the Jews." A long silence follows. "I am well aware of the old prophecies of these people. And every few years a wild man will come out of the desert and claim to be the Messiah. He manages to raise a rabble of followers, but when they discover that his bag of tricks is just that - tricks - they soon leave him, and he wanders back into the wilderness. Or he manages to make a nuisance of himself and gets arrested and crucified." Still the Wise Men say nothing.

"What makes you think that a king has been born right now?" Herod demands with some irritation.

"We have seen a Star in the heavens and have followed it here," Father speaks gently.

"And what's so special about this Star?" Herod, with a slight sneer in his voice.

"The fact that it suddenly appeared and grew steadily for almost a year. Then it stopped. Unlike the other stars in the sky, which move with the seasons of the year, this one has stayed in the same place the whole time."

"And where is this star tonight?" Asks Herod, as he gets up from his couch and unsteadily walks toward a great arched window. He stumbles and lurches against my couch. Putting out a hand to keep from falling, he leans heavily on me. My reaction is immediate and startling: I jump to my feet, staring at Herod as if he is an apparition. With a cry of sheer horror, I turn and run from the room. Josias follows me.

"My Lord, King, please forgive my son. He did not mean to insult you in any way!"

"Wa's his problem!" Herod shouts, his speech slurred with wine.

Chapter Twenty-five - Visiting Herod

"He must have been dreaming my Lord, and when you touched him, you did not wake him all the way. The young are that way sometimes. They do not wake up all the way." Seeing rage building in Herod's face Father speaks quickly and soothingly. After a moment, Herod turns with a shrug.

"What were we talking 'bout?" He staggers a step or two. "Oh, yes, the Star. Where'sit?"

"There, my Lord," Gandophares draws him to the window, guiding him past several inert bodies. "See, my Lord, how brightly it shines?"

"Yes," Herod lets out his breath slowly. And for a moment he senses a deep peace, but it is illusive. "So," he says. "This is s'posed to herald the birth of a Jewish king. Well, you'll not find him in this palace," he swings his arm wide to include everything. "Or any other in the land, for that matter."

He turns away and, feeling his way along the wall, moves toward the throne room. The Magi follow.

"'Cording to my scribes," he continues. "This child's to be born in Bethl'em of Judea. Your Star's hangin' in the sky pretty close to Bethl'em. So, Bal'zar, take your friends an' go pay homage to this king. But!" He wags his finger at Balthazar. "When you find him, come back and tell me where's he at."

"Very well, my Lord, King," Father bows as do the others, taking this as a dismissal.

"Because," adds the King, slyly. "I wanna go an' worship him, m'self." He collapses onto his throne.

Chapter Twenty-Six
Visions

The returning procession moves quietly, winding its way through the silent streets of the sleeping city. The camels' bells have been removed, so the only sound they make is the whisper of their leather feet against the cobblestones. It's unusual, but they are silent when they enter the camp and are told to kneel to let the rider's off and be unsaddled.

Father comes looking for me. He finds me sitting outside my tent, staring into the coals of a dying fire.

"Basilikos," he sits beside me. "Would you like to talk about it?"

"He's evil."

"Why do you say that?" I'm aware that the others have joined us, but my eyes stay riveted on the fire.

"I saw inside him. He's black." I shake my head. "Not the black of a moon-less night, but a foul as a rubbish heap. Snakes writhed in his gut." My voice is low and choked with emotion. "He plans to kill the baby." I finally look at him. "But you know that."

"I didn't think he planned to throw a welcoming party," Father, gruffly. Brushing that aside, he changes the subject. "A little bit before that, you were looking into the fire. What were you seeing?"

"I saw many visions. Some were pleasant enough," I shifted, straightening my back and looking into the night. "Crowds of people mingling and laughing. They settle as soon as a man begins to speak. He's dressed in white with long soft brown hair. The children run to him freely and he hugs them, laughing and stroking their heads.

"But. Then the vision changed. The crowd grows angry and frightened. They begin to shout, to scream, some in anger, some in fear, some in anguish." I shake my head.

The King is Born

"Thank you, Father, for releasing me to sleep." Cheng Sherong and Gandophares look at each other in surprise.

"I saw you were distressed," Father. "But when Herod fell against you, what did you see then? I believe it is important, or I would not make you relive it."

"I know, Father," I glance at him with a tight smile, then return to studying the coals. "But before that. Before you released me to sleep, I saw another night of revelry in that Hall where we were tonight. It is darker and smokier than tonight. The music is erotic, the dancers more seductive with less clothing. One of the dancers, a pretty young woman, not much more than a girl, dances up to Herod." I stop, closing my eyes as if that would erase the memory. I'm ashamed of the feelings that vision aroused. "I'd rather not describe what they did."

"We can imagine, if we want to. Go on."

"Herod is pleased with her and tells her she can have anything she wants. She whispers in his ear. He pushes her away and looks horrified, but then she returns to him and after a few more moments, he gives in and shouts an order to his guards. The whole scene changes. It's dark - black, like a starless night. There's the clanging and banging of iron gates and smoking torches appear. The air is putrid. Men - soldiers - roughly handle a man, yelling profanities at him and laughing, making jokes about Herod and the girl. They force him to lie down on a bench and cut his head off."

I hear the grunts of all three men. Father touches my shoulder. I ignore him. I'm not finished.

"Then I'm back in the Great Hall. The girl is still entertaining Herod. There is another woman with them. An older woman, but very beautiful. The soldiers come in carrying a huge platter. I wonder what they'd be serving this late in the evening. Then I see what is on the platter: The man's head."

I jump up and run into the shadows, retching. Those left behind hang their heads, waiting in silence. When I feel able to go on, I return to my cushion.

"Was that all you saw?" Father.

"Balthazar, he's gone through enough!" Cries Gandophares.

"No more, man!" Cheng Sherong protests.

Chapter Twenty-Six - Visions

"I agree," Father nods. "But I believe there is more, and I believe we must hear it."

"Yes. That vision is of a time in the future. I could tell because Herod looked much older and more ... degenerated - grossly fat, greasy hair, slobbering lips. That was the vision Father released me from. But then, later, when Herod fell on me, I saw an instant reality even now happening. It made the beheading seem like child's play." I frown at the embers. "I can't put it into words as I did the other, I can only describe the impressions."

"Go ahead," Father urges.

"I hear women screaming, wailing. Men sobbing. Children screaming. Babies crying. I see moving swords, moonlight reflecting off black liquid dripping from them. Dark pools on light colored cobblestones. Bloodied garments. Dead babies, hacked in pieces. Women holding parts of their babies, some trying to put them back together. Blood everywhere!" I drop my head on my arms and begin to sob. Father gathers me to him and holds me tightly against his chest. I can feel his body shaking. Gandophares and Cheng Sherong sit staring into the coals, their grim faces streaked with tears.

"We must go at once," Gandophares.

"Yes," agrees Cheng Sherong. I feel Father nod. I can hear the others moving about, calling urgently, but quietly to the servants.

༺♥༻

The rising sun finds our small group moving quickly along the road to Bethlehem. The distance is not great and by mid-morning, we arrive outside Bethlehem. Father rides next to me, holding the reigns of my camel as I am asleep in my howdah, a bench-like affair shaded by a canopy that replaces a saddle when needed.

"How's he doing?" Asks Gandophares as he and Cheng Sherong pull up beside Father

"He's sleeping it off," Father in a low voice. "You understand why I had to push him to tell us all he saw."

"Yes," said Cheng Sherong. "It was tough to hear it coming from one so young. He is growing up very fast."

"He has to," says Father. "His is a great destiny that has already begun." They ride in silence.

THE KING IS BORN

"It's obvious we won't be going back to Jerusalem," Gandophares. "How shall we return?"

"Josias has suggested another way home. He said there are other routes we can take from Bethlehem."

"I don't believe Herod will come after us," Gandophares sounds hopeful. "He'll be too busy trying to find the child."

"This is all dangerous," Cheng Sherong is worried.

"I have a different plan," I pipe up. I've been listening to them.

"Basil!" Father, surprised. "What sort of plan?"

"Come closer."

Chapter Twenty-Seven
The Visit

❦❦❦

Gaius and another soldier went into the town to locate the parents of the child. Now they are back with good news.

"My Lord," Gaius, trying to control his excitement. "We have located the parents of the child. As soon as you are ready, we can go."

"Good work! We are ready! Let's leave at once," Father.

Gaius, the other soldier, Arash - aptly named as he is a bear of a man, Josias, another servant and I pick up woven baskets with items that we might be bringing to the market, or that we might have just bought. The Magi's gifts are hidden in three of them.

"It's strange, isn't it?" Gandophares speaks low as we walk through the bustling streets of Bethlehem. "Yesterday we put on all our finery and in pomp and majesty presented ourselves to a king."

"And today we dress as simple travelers. No pomp, no ceremony," Cheng Sherong adds.

"The King doesn't need it," I say, realizing the truth of my words as I say them.

"We're here, my Lords," Gaius says as we turn into a small street and stop at an open Carpenter's workshop where a man is working on a piece of furniture.

"Joseph!" Gaius calls to the man. "We've returned with the Magi as we promised."

Joseph wipes his hands on his leather apron and approaches the Wise Men.

"Welcome, my Lords!" We all bow. "If you will step inside, please, I will close the shop."

Gaius and Arash help Joseph shut and bar the doors. Joseph guides them through the dimness to a back door, opening onto a

The King is Born

small courtyard with a shaded arbor at one end to which he leads us.

"Thank you, sir," Father speaks while Joseph lays out a rug before us. "You do not seem surprised to see us."

"We have received many visitors for the child, my Lord," Joseph. "Nothing has been the same since he was born."

The door to the house opens and a woman steps out, carrying a child about two years old. She wears a shawl over her head, but her face is not covered. She bows her head in recognition of us and places the child on the rug on the floor. The baby looks at the wall of feet around him, then tips his head back attempting to look into our faces. His mother catches him as he starts to topple over. We immediately kneel or sit on the rug around him. The baby laughs, clapping his hands in delight. Then he gets up and toddles toward Father. Father holds out his arms, but the baby clambers into his lap, sitting with his back against Father's chest. He pulls Father's sleeves, drawing Father's arms around himself. He leans his head back and kicks his feet in the air and laughs. He twists around to look up into Father's face and strokes his beard. Father bends his head, and the baby kisses his cheek, then pushes Father's arms apart and scrambles off his lap. As Father steadies him, I see a tear slide down his cheek.

The child goes next to Gandophares. Gandophares put his arms out as Father had and again the child ignores them and climbs into his lap. Again, he leans against the man's chest for a moment or two before standing facing Gandophares. He lays his chubby little hands on Gandophares' cheeks and looks long into his eyes. He nods with a smile and kisses his cheek.

Next comes Cheng Sherong who is openly weeping. The baby wipes the tears from his cheek, then stands on tiptoe and kisses Cheng Sherong full on the lips. Cheng Sherong wraps his arms around the child, burying his face in the folds of the child's tunic. After a very long time, he lets the child go. Now he's smiling as he looks into the child's face. The child smiles back.

Yeshua moves on to Josias who holds his arms out and, with a chortle of delight, he runs into them, throwing his arms around Josias' neck. Gaius and Arash get similar treatment and the four play together like long-lost brothers.

Chapter Twenty-Seven - The Visit

"Forgive us for coming without announcing ourselves," Father speaks quietly so as not to disturb those playing. "My name is Balthazar, and this is Gandophares and Cheng Sherong and my son, Basilikos. My servant, Josias, is one of your people. We have come a long way to see this child and to bring gifts to him. We are Magi - High Priests of the Temples of our people in Persia, China and India. We are also Astrologers and have each seen the Star from our own lands. It first appeared about two and a half years ago in the southwestern sky. It grew and grew until it was so large that it outshone the moon. Then it stopped growing and stayed still. That was when we began our journey, for we believed that a king had been born. More than a king - The King, the Savior, the Messiah."

"Many have come to see him," whispers his mother.

"My wife's name is Mary, and I am Joseph. And the baby's name is Jesus, or, Yeshua."

They continue to talk together until Yeshua comes back to his mother and leans against her.

The baskets with the gifts in them are sorted out and placed beside each Wise Man. Gandophares presents his gift first.

"I bring Frankincense. In our beliefs it is a deity in itself. Its fragrance is unparalleled and every part of it is usable. In is the only incense worthy of a king." He places the ornate box in front of Yeshua and opens it. The fragrance soon fills the air. Yeshua claps his hands. His babbling filled with giggles and laughter as he takes deep sniffs of the fragrant air.

Cheng Sherong unwraps his gift.

"I bring him a crown made of the purest of gold, for only this is worthy of a King to wear." He places the crown before Yeshua who picks it up and tries to put it on his head. It falls onto his shoulders and slides down his arms, holding them against his sides. Mary quickly lifts it off of him. Yeshua touches the gems mounted on its surface and oohs.

Father hesitates to present his gift. I feel for him as I remember the discussion we had earlier about it. But Yeshua turns to him and waits. All merriment has gone, and his little face is serious as he looks up to Father.

The King is Born

"My gift," he sighs, "is one that even I do not completely understand." He places a flask on the rug in front of Yeshua. Yeshua stares at it, then reaches for it with one finger, drawing it back quickly as if it is burned. He tucks his fists under his armpits and steps back against his mother. He looks up at Father who makes no effort to hide his tears. Yeshua goes to him and kisses his cheek, patting him as if trying to comfort him.

After a minute or so, he turns away from Father and comes to me. He holds his arms up to be picked up. I lift him onto my lap and sniff, wiping the tears off my own face. Yeshua notices with interest but doesn't respond.

Ruby, dislodged as I bent to pick Yeshua up, sparkles against my tunic, drawing Yeshua' attention as I attempt to speak.

"I, I'm sorry, I don't have a gift – I didn't know – I…"

"The Savior has come!" Ruby's voice rings with joy.

Yeshua picks up Ruby, cupping her in his little hands, and turns her to the light.

Ruby seems to absorb the light, drawing it into her depths. For a moment, all is still. Suddenly a red light begins to flow out of her, filling the arbor, spilling through the lattice and down the step into the yard. It fills that, and keeps rising until it overflows the rooftops, spreading across the hills and valleys. And still it flows, up into the heavens until all is bathe in the red light.

Then, as if in reverse motion, the light begins to return - but not into Ruby - It flows into the little body in my arms. Yeshua absorbs it all, and for a moment all is still. Then the light reappears and surrounds me, but it's different. It has a liquid quality to it. A liquid red light. I close my eyes and feel my body absorb the light.

I tremble with the shock of it. As my vision clears, I am looking across the hills. The air is clear, but where ever I look, objects are translucent and filled with the liquid red light.

I turn to look into the child's eyes. Those ancient, all-knowing eyes hold a question. I unclasp Ruby's chain and close the little hands around her.

" This is Ruby. She has come to be such a close friend and companion. She is like my own heart to me. I give you this heart as a token of my heart that is forever yours."

Chapter Twenty-Seven - The Visit

Yeshua presses Ruby to his own heart and smiles into my eyes.

༺♡༻

"We bring bad news with us," Father turns to Mary and Joseph, speaking quietly. "We did not know where to go to find the child. We assumed He would be born in the palace in Jerusalem and so that was where we went first. But no one knew about His birth. When we did get an audience with King Herod, it was obvious that our inquiries upset him. He told us to return and tell him where the child was, so that he could come and worship Him too. But, well, we believe that he plans to try and kill the child."

"I had a dream last night," Joseph matches the tone of Father's voice. "An Angel of the Lord told me to leave immediately, that the child's life was in danger. We were planning to go as soon as the town has settled for the night."

"How and where would you go?" Father.

"Well, I guess to Egypt. I have distant family in a small town there. I think I could find them and that they would take us in. I am a good carpenter and will earn my keep."

"Will you trust us to help you get away safely?" Cheng Sherong.

Mary and Joseph exchanged glances.

"Our caravan is stopped just outside the town's gates," said Gandophares. "Although we did not come in the pomp we had intended, as the child deserves, people did see us come to visit you. When we leave, we will make sure they will also see us go. You will be with us - there's safety in numbers."

"But if we go with you, they will see us!" Mary in angst.

"Not if they think that you are our servants. Mary, you must dress as a man. I am sorry, but we have no women in our caravan, and you would look conspicuous. We have brought robes for you both so that you will match our servants. You can place the Baby in one of the baskets we brought. Two of our servants will stay here and leave after dark."

"You put yourselves at great risk. Why?" Mary, a little suspicious.

THE KING IS BORN

"That is why we are here." I join them carrying Yeshua. "That is why I came after Father. I didn't know what danger threatened the child, but that he, and all with him were in danger. At Herod's dinner I discovered his intent. Joseph's dream confirms it." Mary takes Yeshua from me, looking first into his face then at me.

"Where are the clothes?"

Chapter Twenty-Eight
The Escape

∽♥♥∾

Father and Gandophares lead. Cheng Sherong and I follow. We walk leisurely, chatting as we go. Josias, another servant, Mary and Joseph walk behind us. Each carries some sort of filled basket. Joseph's basket holds Yeshua covered by clothing. Gaius and Arash bring up the rear.

The group walks through the streets without hurrying. Mary tries to stride like the men, panic only seconds away. I drop back beside her.

"You are doing well. Your behavior is excellent. You're only a boy, so don't try to take big strides. It's alright to act as if your basket is heavy, and that you are frightened, as would a boy servant would also be a bit frightened of being reprimanded." I pat her shoulder. "Just don't work at it quite so hard, hmm?" She nods with an attempt at a smile and hefts her basket up under her arm.

We reach the marketplace and spread out, stopping at each booth.

"Good day, moocher (vendor)," I begin. "Sir, if you have a male child two years or younger, get him out of the town right away. Soldiers are coming with orders to kill all boys two or younger. Do it now, sir!" The man's face blanches. He turns to a woman in the back of his stall. I move on to the next stall.

We finally can see the city gates and are about to head toward them when Ruby calls to me.

"Basil! The soldiers are at the gates!" Ruby calls to me from her new position against Yeshua' chest.

"Soldiers!" Gaius says as he strides past me.

"How do we get them out of here?" I ask.

"There are other ways out of the city not commonly known." Joseph pauses beside me, too. "Tell the people to get out by them

THE KING IS BORN

and hide in the hills until the soldiers are gone! Follow me!"

As we hurry without hurrying, Joseph shouts to the people in their own language. He turns down a side street. Gaius stops and leans against a corner wall. We begin to move in his direction when we are caught.

"Halt!" A soldier shouts as he and two others approach us. "Where are you going?"

"I go about my own business." Father responds in Latin with a smile and a wave of the hand.

"What is your name?!" The soldier does the same.

"I am Jenghiz Madjidius," Says father, majestically.

"You are not dressed like a Roman!"

Father laughs. "In this heat?! One would be mad to wear a woolen toga here!"

"And these others?"

"My son and my nephew are Roman, of course. Jenghiz Madjidius Basilikos and Jenghiz Madjidius Gaius." He turns to the others with a wide grin. "I do not suppose to insult you by claiming these two are Romans! This is Kong from China and Viraj of India! "

"And you live here?"

"Would you care to come with me to my home for some light refreshments?" Father bows with a sweep of his arm past the street where Gaius waits. The soldier ignores him.

"Do you know any woman who has given birth to a boy child in the last two years?"

Father feigns surprise. "No, sir! Alas my son is my only boy child. Now girls! Do you need a woman? I have many daughters to choose from!"

The soldiers laugh, saying something about another time, and return to their hunt. We casually turn down the street with Gaius, searching for Josias' row of stone telling us which way to go. Turning the first corner, we break into a run. After another turn, we hear women's voices and run towards them along the outer wall of the town and come upon a crowd of jostling, frantic women attempting to get through a small arch in the wall. Josias is trying to sort them out with little effect.

Chapter Twenty-Eight - The Escape

Gaius and Arash run to his aide.

"Gaius, go through the arch and help the women out and over the stream and on their way!"

I go with him, helping the nearest woman and child through the arch, and across the stream. As I let her go and turn back, Gaius passes another to me.

Inside the wall, Arash and the Magi sort out the women and get them into an orderly line. More men join them. Silence descends as people move quickly, happy to have order restored and someone to give directions.

Mary and Yeshua are handed to me. I help them up the bank and start to say something when a man approaches me.

"You are with Mary and the baby?" I frown and hesitate.

"Go! Go with them! We will send Joseph and the Magi after you shortly!"

I scramble up the bank and hurry with Mary into the shelter of a line of olive trees. We reach a valley strewn with boulders and settle behind one, waiting for the others to join us.

The heat and glare of the sun is almost unbearable. Yeshua is fussy. Mary tries to nurse him, but he isn't interested. I draw him into the little shade I make and begin to play games with him.

The sun drops behind the hill and the relief is palatable.

"Your Father is coming with the rest of the men!" Ruby calls out.

Yeshua jumps up calling for his father who appears around the boulder, the Wise Men close behind. Joseph lifts and swings around with him, making him chortle. Then Joseph reaches for Mary. We step away.

⁂

As night fell, Joseph led us further into the valley and up onto the hilltop. From here we can hear the sounds of the carnage in the town.

"Basil, Gaius is looking for you!" Ruby calls to me.

"Where is he, Ruby?"

"On the other side of the hill you're on!"

The King is Born

I scramble over the hill and make the call of an owl. After a moment, I hear a similar call. I stand and Gaius steps into the starlight. We hug and whisper our pleasure of being together again.

"The camels are a little further on." Gaius whispers

"Is Nicias with them?"

"No. As we were leaving Jerusalem, your father asked him to take word to Captain Ahmed to start the main caravan toward home. I have a contingent of fighting men, plus servants and enough camels for all of us."

A commotion in the valley draws us back over the hill. A light of torches is bobbing toward the valley, some already spreading out as soldiers search for the women and babies. The awful sounds begin again.

There's no easy way out of the valley for the women but to climb the rugged slopes.

"Dear God!" I groan. "We've led them into a trap!"

"Some are already over the hill and others are following!" Ruby calls. "We must hurry, Basil!" I reach for the pendant, forgetting I gave it to Yeshua. I suddenly feel very vulnerable.

"Look!" Whispers Gaius, pointing at shifting shadows on the slopes opposite us. I grab his arm, pulling him over the hill to gather our people. As quietly as we can, we crawl up and over the hilltop, breaking into a run once out of sight of the valley behind us.

The camels are kneeling, waiting for us. Mine still has the howdah on it, so we lift Mary and Yeshua into it. Joseph will ride beside them. We mount, raise the camels and head west, riding through the night and day.

Just before sunset on the third day, Gaius calls a halt at a small, unused oasis.

"I believe we are far enough now that we can rest here for the night. Both the camels and humans badly need it!"

We set up a small tent for the family and the rest of us settle in a circle around it. The camels are tethered close in. One man stands guard. But as exhausted as we all are, even the guard succumbs to sleep.

"Basil! Wake up!" Ruby's voice is like an annoying fly,

Chapter Twenty-Eight - The Escape

buzzing in my head.

"*Go way, Ruby!!*" I grumble.

"*BASIL!*" She shouts. I didn't know she could shout! "*Horsemen coming!*"

I'm wide awake.

I scramble to find Father and shake him. "Ruby says horsemen are approaching!"

Father finds it hard to wake up, so I shake the others and repeat the warning.

"*Basil!*" Ruby again. "*It's Mongke!*"

I swing round, searching the shadows. The light of the stars and moon is bright, making the shadows black and concealing.

"*Mongke? Where are you?*" I'm afraid to speak out loud, hoping he will hear me as Ruby does.

A shadow breaks away from the deeper shadows and draws near. I recognize Mongke, greeting him with a hug and a slap on the back.

"Quiet, Basil. Soldiers have been following you! They are only about eight furlongs away."

"We are exposed! What can we do?"

"Basilikos, who is this man?" Father comes up behind me.

"Shhhhh! Father, this is Mongke. Mongke, Balthazar, Cheng Sherong and Gandophares. Mongke says we are being followed!"

"We are exposed!" Father whispers, glancing around.

"Basil, did you see me before I stood up?" Mongke also whispers.

"No! I had no idea any one was near, except for Ruby's warning."

"Exactly!" Mongke turns to the others who have joined us. "Gaius, get the tent down and bury it! Josias, have the servants move the camels behind those large rocks there. Keep them quiet! The rest of you, get behind these rocks as well!"

We do as we are told and huddle behind the rocks.

"Thank the Mighty One the camels are quiet!" Whispers Father.

The King is Born

"They know Who is among them, and they know the danger." Mongke.

"The camels do?" I ask, bewildered. Mongke nods. *"Well, why not! I don't think anything will surprise me anymore!"*

The creak of saddle leather stops any thought of conversation.

On the other side of the rocks several soldiers on horseback stop and dismount. The Centurion squats and studies the sand.

"They were here! And not long ago!" He rises. "We will push on. They cannot be that far ahead of us now!"

"Do you still believe they are headed for Egypt?" One of the soldiers asks.

"Where else would they be headed going south by west?!"

"Could we make camp and rest here for a few hours? The horses need it even if we don't."

The Centurion slaps his gloves against the palm of his hands. "We ride!"

As the sounds recede, we move out from behind the rocks.

"That was close!" Gaius mutters, then a little more confidently, "Once more, Mongke, you've saved us!"

"You are not completely clear yet!" Mongke. "I will stay with you for a while, in case they return, or other dangers threaten."

"Should we move on now, or stay here and rest?" Father has joined us.

"Stay and rest, all of you. We will stand watch." He moves away, melting into the shadows. We join the others behind the rocks and settle to sleep.

⁓♥⁓

Mongke and his men have stayed with us as we traveled around the northern end of the Red Sea and entered Egypt.

The next morning, he stops beside me.

"Basil, I have to return to my own country."

"You're leaving us?" Panic surges. He grips my shoulder.

"You are safe now as you are not known in these parts. Joseph's hometown is a day's easy riding from here. You will be fine!"

Chapter Twenty-Eight - The Escape

"I've rather grown used to you being with us."

"I know. I wish I could stay, but for reasons you cannot understand, I must go now. I have stayed much longer than I was supposed to. But. We will meet again, I promise!" He grins and accepts my hug, then strides away.

I go in search of Father to let him know we are now on our own.

"He left just like that? With all his men?" Father is non-plussed. "How strange! Well. We'll just have to manage without him, I suppose." We inform the others and shortly get on our way south. Joseph is obviously relieved to be so close to the end of the journey.

୬୦୨୦

We stayed a few days with them to make sure that they will be all right, and that Herod's troops had not followed us. Now it's time for us to return to Madjid. We will travel in the cool of the night, moving fast in order to catch up with Nicias and the rest of the caravan.

Mary and Joseph and Yeshua have come with us to the outskirts of town. The sun is close to the western horizon. "I don't know how we can ever thank you," says Mary to Father. "What you have done is . . ."

"Don't! Please, Mary," Father hugs her and Yeshua. "Basilikos told you, we were meant to be here. It is all part of the story. It is all prophesied." He looks down at her and the child in her arms. "I only wish I could do more," he strokes Yeshua's head.

"I wish you could stay," on a sniff. "I feel safe with all of you here."

"It's not going to be easy; you know that." I'm standing close to them and feel I must warn her.

"I'm sure it won't."

"His life is going to be a strange one." Father. "The life of a prophet, sage and teacher is hard – hardest on those he loves most, I believe." He pats my shoulder. "We tend to have a one-track mind and forget completely that there are other things that need to be done, or other people – especially our own. And the prophecies about your son," He stops, seeing the pain on her face.

The King is Born

"Mary," he continues gently. "I pray God gives you the strength when you need it." He gathers her back into his arms and holds her as he would his own daughter. She rests in his arms as she would her father's. Yeshua snuggles between them, then pushes them apart, holding his arms out to me.

I take him and start to hug him. " What is it, Yeshua? I'm going to miss you so much!" But he pushes away from me and pulls something out of his little tunic. Light sparks off Ruby's facets.

"Ruby? You want me to take back Ruby?"

Yeshua nods.

"Well, you do have my true heart anyway." I return him to Mary and hang Ruby around my neck, tucking her under my own tunic.

Yeshua reaches over and pats my chest with a smile. "Keep safe!"

"I will!" Startled, I realize he is talking to Ruby to keep me safe! I start to say something, but the others are already mounting their camels. I hurry to follow suite.

"Go in peace," Joseph raises a hand and Yeshua copies him.

"And that, Dillwyn, is how Basil rescued the King." Ruby says as I watch a dozen camels, ten with riders and two without, move off, heading east into the darkening desert. The image on the wall fades away.

"What happens next? Do they get home in time to save Madjid?"

"Dillwyn, you can hardly keep your eyes open!"

"I'll make some tea!" I rise and head for the door.

"I could keep going, but I think you'd miss most of it! Another time I will show you what happens on the trip home and more. Now, go to bed!"

About the Author - Marian Webb Betts

I was born in Sudan, and spent my first 13 years in the back of beyond. With no communication from the outside world, few books except the KJV Bible and the Golden Bells Hymnbook, our entertainment was based on Dad's innate ability to tell a good story – of his hair-raising adventures among people whose only experience with white men was with slave traders. He also made up stories about the wild animals and the different tribes with which we lived.

Toys, too, were scarce, too. The native children taught us how to make clay people and animals which we used in re-enacting Dad's stories and making up our own.

My father was an English Professor and my mother a published poet. They taught us proper Queen's English. We also learned Basque French and Egyptian Arabic. Growing up speaking, writing and reading in three very different languages caused more than one conundrum when we immigrated to the USA where "English" had a whole different vocabulary!

Eventually I put my early years' learning to use, expanding my storytelling with paint, fabric and photography.

Now I own my own Studio and Publishing Company having designed book jackets and illustrations for many books, articles, technical papers and "How-To" guides, The latest adventure is expanding the Legends of Ruby Heart for my own pleasure and for those who enjoy imagining "what if?"

I originally wrote the first three stories in one book that ended up being close to four hundred pages and was too expensive to publish and sell. So I divided the three stories, updating them as I go to form a trilogy. THE KING IS BORN is the first. THE BETWEEN YEARS will be out shortly. And Ruby isn't finished yet: She has many more Guardians whose stories are yet to come!

www.ingramcontent.com/pod-product-compliance
Lightning Source LLC
LaVergne TN
LVHW021237080526
838199LV00088B/4560